"This is possibly the mos

writer I've ever read. A
crystals, the stories are
with uncomfortable subject matter, like rape, or challenging characters, like a self-mutilating, sexually precocious girl. But this is a writer who takes risks. This is the kind of book that will get under your skin because the author herself has spent devoted hours under her characters'."

—Alfian Sa'at, author of *Malay Sketches*

"Witty and wonderfully inventive."

—Clarissa Oon, *The Straits Times*

"Populated by a diverse and unexpected cast of characters—from maids to Maria Hertogh to the Merlion—Lee Koe's collection of fourteen stories questions, changes or expands many accepted notions, myths and memories of Singapore. And it does so in remarkably hip and inventive prose."

—Helmi Yusof, *The Business Times*

"Authors such as Amanda Lee Koe are beginning to forge a distinctive literary voice for the city-state; her debut collection of short stories addresses questions of Singaporean identity, national memory and myth-making. Lee Koe resists happy endings, and, across several stories, lovers or potential lovers end up separated, or reunited only when it is too late for love to flourish. But despite the gloom, in *Ministry of Moral Panic* are moving testaments to fractured, or unorthodox, lives."

—Rosie Milne, *Asian Review of Books*

"Amanda Lee Koe is mesmerising. Her characters sleepwalk out of a Haruki Murakami novel, across the forgotten set of a Wong Kar-wai film, before nestling in a subway with warm paninis of lust, hysteria, anomie, dissonance and fresh lettuce. One of the finest writers in her generation."

—Daren Shiau, author of *Heartland*

"A magnificent collection of short stories that are as formally innovative as they are profoundly human, compassionate and insightful."

—Huzir Sulaiman, author of *Eight Plays*

"Amanda Lee Koe's melancholic, often heartbreaking tales of urban malaise are elegies of individual yearnings. At her best, tides of words flow like movements of music, their cadences aspiring towards the magic of poetry. In this debut collection, the author has distinguished herself as a competent, lyrical raconteur."

—Sam Ng, *Quarterly Literary Review Singapore*

"There is nothing staid or predictable about an Amanda Lee Koe story, and readers expecting another local writer waxing lyrical about the everyday intricacies of HDB life will be pleasantly disappointed. Each story is inventive in its own way, and showcases her astute observational powers and flair for writing in equal parts. They break the mould of ones set in Singapore and dealing with Singaporeans, and look set to inspire a new generation of writers by changing their perception of what local short stories can be."

—Jennani Durai, *The Straits Times*

"It's tempting to label Lee Koe a Singaporean Murakami. Her stories, while set in our very familiar city-state, transcend time and space. Clearly, she's forging not just a distinctive literary voice for Singapore's contemporary condition, but also a different path for a new generation of writers who will take Singapore fiction to its next chapter."

—Pamela Ho, *The A List*

"There is a deftness of touch, a sureness of intent, a knowingness of accomplishment that makes it hard to believe that *Ministry of Moral Panic* is Amanda Lee Koe's first book of fiction. She has marked out in virgin territory a realm of her own, a kingdom of weird, non-conforming, stubborn passions in Singapore. And she has done so without resorting to the usual pieties of understanding and tolerance. She has looked directly at the contorted subject and drawn every contortion that she could see…the collection is eminently readable. I should know. I read it straight through—all fourteen stories—on my flight from Singapore to New York. I had not been able to read on a plane for a while. Too uncomfortable and distracted. But these stories carried me to the end."

—Jee Leong Koh, author of *The Pillow Book*

"I finished this book in one sitting. It is—for the lack of a better adjective—*unputdownable.* Evocative and inventive, Amanda brings something new and original to the Singaporean literature scene. She paints her characters so vividly; honest, raw and flawed. Her characters are displayed as quintessentially Singaporean, and that they are also nonconformists, in a sense. They are not merely two-dimensional—they possess a rich layer of personality, with real dreams and desires."

—Humairah, *The Book Jacket*

"No other work I have read in the last two years has bent my head around in such uncomfortable knots, while simultaneously giving off the comforting aroma of familiarity. It pulls off the contortionist act of being dreadfully Singaporean and unSingaporean at the same time—every story, every sentence is in its improper place."

—Joshua Ip, author of *Making Love with Scrabble Tiles*

"Exciting, surprising, and so unpredictable in the sense that the stories are never formulaic. At the same time, they are filled with people who get under your skin and move you with their familiar yet eerie tendencies."

—Lydia Kwa, author of Pulse

"It really is an incredible collection—the settings of the stories will be deeply familiar to Singaporeans, and yet the emotional territories they explore are vast, and their conclusions devastating."

—Ng Yi-Sheng, author of *Last Boy*

"Fittingly enough, *Ministry of Moral Panic*, just like the city of gardens, is an exciting collection of beginnings, with uncertain endings far ahead."

—Ho Lin, *Your Impossible Voice*

"Once in a while, a book excites me so much that I can't get over the excitement to sit down and continue reading. This is one of them. It is one of the best works in Singapore today and highly recommended."

—Oh Yong Hwee, author of *Ten Sticks and One Rice*

Amanda Lee Koe is the fiction editor of *Esquire (Singapore)*, editor of creative non-fiction platform *Poskod.sg*, and a 2013 Honorary Fellow of the International Writing Program at the University of Iowa. With Ng Yi-Sheng, she spearheaded and co-edited *Eastern Heathens*, an anthology subverting Asian folklore. Her writing has been published in seven countries. She is currently an MFA candidate at Columbia University's Writing Program, where she is working on her first novel, and splits her time between New York City and Singapore.

STORIES

AMANDA LEE KOE

EPIGRAM BOOKS / SINGAPORE

Published in Singapore by Epigram Books
www.epigrambooks.sg

Edited by Jason Erik Lundberg

These pieces were originally published (in slightly different form) in the following places:

"Flamingo Valley", *Bellevue Literary Review*, Fall 2013
"Pawn", *Quarterly Literary Review Singapore*, Vol. 12, No. 3, July 2013
"The King of Caldecott Hill", *Quarterly Literary Review Singapore*, Vol. 12, No. 4, October 2013
"Love Is No Big Truth", *Cha: An Asian Literary Journal*, March 2013
"Laundromat", *From the Belly of the Cat*, Math Paper Press, October 2013
"Siren", *Eastern Heathens*, Ethos Books, March 2013

National Library Board, Singapore
Cataloguing-in-Publication Data

Lee Koe, Amanda, 1987-
Ministry of moral panic : stories / Amanda Lee Koe. – Singapore : Epigram Books, 2013.
p. cm

ISBN: 978-981-07-5732-8 (paperback)
ISBN: 978-981-07-5733-5 (ebook)

I. Title.

PR9570.S53
S823 -- dc23 OCN855509308

With thanks to Amelia Ng, Wei Fen Lee and Wei-Ling Woo—ALK

First Edition: October 2013

10 9 8 7

For Bud,
left standing.

Was it Laurie Anderson who said that VR would never look real until they learned how to put some dirt in it? Singapore's airport, the Changi Airtropolis, seemed to possess no more resolution than some early VPL world. There was no dirt whatsoever; no muss, no furred fractal edge to things. Outside, the organic, florid as ever in the tropics, had been gardened into brilliant green, and all-too-perfect examples of itself. Only the clouds were feathered with chaos—weird columnar structures towering above the Strait of China.

The cab driver warned me about littering. He asked where I was from.

He asked if it was clean there. "Singapore very clean city." One of those annoying Japanese-style mechanical bells cut in as he exceeded the speed limit, just to remind us both that he was doing it. There seemed to be golf courses on either side of the freeway . . .

"You come for golf?"

"No."

"Business?"

"Pleasure."

He sucked his teeth. He had his doubts about that one.

— William Gibson, "Disneyland with the Death Penalty", *Wired*, 1993

CONTENTS

Flamingo Valley

LING KO MUI, the hot fuss of Flamingo Valley, the old Malay man says. Oh ho, you still gots it, don't you, baby.

All the old Chinese men and women turn up their yellow wrinkled faces like sea turtles, and Deddy Haikel gives a flourish that looks like *shazam*. Ling Ko Mui creaks her gaze tentatively toward him.

Yes, you! Deddy Haikel says, I'm talking to you, girl, but her clouded eyes have swivelled back to the television set, where some Mandarin travel show is playing.

Didn't you ask me to take you for a ride on my motorbike?

Didn't you come see me play the National Theatre?

Didn't your Chinese boyfriend beat me up on Bencoolen Street?

It's *Deddy Haikel*!

He picks up his guitar, which is never ever too far away, and begins strumming the first few chords of 'Barbara Shimmies on Bugis Street'. His voice isn't like it was any more, not since the throat operation, but it reaches into Ling Ko Mui and she looks up at him, her squinting eyes almost meeting his.

The woman is *nyanyuk*, one of the old Chinese men croaks to Deddy Haikel, twirling a finger beside his temple. Doesn't remember anything. Can't even recognise her daughter.

Deddy Haikel lets the riff sag, props a leg on a chair and

says, Hey, this whole ward is the *nyanyuk* ward, isn't it? Don't think you're so smart. You're soft in the head too. He turns back to Ling Ko Mui, but she has averted her eyes, in exactly the same manner as when she was eighteen and he asked her for a dance.

There are things that cut through swathes of memory, there are things you take with you that are non-essential, that drag you down, but you can't offload them because there is only one way to throw them overboard and that is for you to walk the plank.

• • •

He'd finished his set in the small pub, covers of the Rolling Stones and the Beatles, played on a guitar he'd saved up a year and a half to purchase, delivering newspapers on weekends. He'd skipped school to see Cliff Richards & the Shadows at Happy World in 1961 and could there be anything better?

He'd come off the small raised platform and was making his way to the bar. The pub, popular with British servicemen, was a short distance away from the barracks. In the mass of khaki uniforms, there was a young Chinese girl in a full white skirt, prim on a bar stool. He wondered if she was here with someone—it was rare to see girls out alone in the evenings, much less in bars. When he reached the bar she turned.

You're very good, she said.

Thank you. Do you come here often?

My father owns the pub. We live upstairs.

It must get noisy.

It does, but I love music. The only thing I don't understand is why it's always only the Eurasians and you Malays. We don't ever have Chinese musicians coming in to play.

He laughed. You Chinese are too busy trying to be businessmen. Making real money.

That's sad.

Nah, it's how the world works—it's how your father can give me five dollars for playing tonight's set.

Listen, I'm starving—will you take me to eat? I saw that you ride a motorbike. I've never been on one.

Sure. What would you like to eat?

Surprise me. As long as we get there on your motorbike.

• • •

They sat across a rickety aluminium table at a kedai makan, platters of nasi kandar and sup kambing between them. Ling Ko Mui picked up a fork and spoon. Deddy Haikel considered the cutlery briefly, then reached in with his right hand as he normally would.

Is there a technique?

To?

To eating with your hands?

He showed her how to gather the rice into a loose ball, packing it more tightly as he went along. She imitated him with her own hands.

Only with your right hand.

Why?

Well . . . the left is unclean.

I could wash it.

No, not like that. The right hand is for eating, and the left hand—the left hand is for cleaning your bottom.

Ah, I see.

Do you like the rice?

It's delicious. But why is Malay chilli sweet?

It helps the musicians write better love songs.

• • •

Every Friday evening, he would play the 8–9pm set at the pub owned by Ling Ko Mui's father, and when her father was busy at the counter, they would sneak out for supper on his motorbike—Malay food one week, Chinese food the next. Her father was cordial enough to Deddy Haikel the musician, but Deddy Haikel the suitor would have been tossed out the back door like the beansprout ends and chicken bones left over from dinner. Over teh halia or hot Horlicks after supper, they would talk about music. She told him he ought to get a backing band, that he ought to write his own songs, that she could help with the lyrics.

Once, he came to the pub an hour earlier. Her parents were at the temple of the Goddess of Mercy, her younger siblings playing catch on the street. They ran upstairs, light-footed, and she drew the curtains together before unearthing her father's record player from under a Chinese silk doily. They crouched close together as he watched her delicate fingers put on an imported Petula Clark record, tuning the volume down. When 'Ya Ya Twist' started playing, Deddy Haikel got to his feet and put out his hand. Ling Ko Mui hesitated, then took it; they danced in the gathering twilight, ceiling fan whirring slowly above them.

She started singing softly with the music as he held her close, and then closer. He loved the sweet, nasal quality to her voice and he closed his eyes, letting his thoughts race through—perhaps she could be a backing vocalist in his band? Would they have a Malay wedding, or a Chinese one? Could he give up the Qur'an for her? Would she give her own parents up for him, the way he was prepared to give his up for her? He wanted to say something, but the record was ending, running empty under the needle. Ling Ko Mui pulled away from him gently, kneeling by the floor to flip the vinyl.

• • •

There was a Chinese girl I was gila in love with, Deddy Haikel says to the young nurse, as she listens to his heartbeat, assessing the damage of this second heart attack. I would have done anything to get into her pants, and it wasn't even about that.

There was a Chinese boy who felt the same way about her. I didn't know about him, but he knew about me. I was walking down Bencoolen Street one day when someone tapped my shoulder. When I turned around, he punched me right in the face. He'd sent his men to do the legwork: they knew I played Friday sets at her father's pub and that I had supper with her after. That she would put her arms on either side of my waist as she rode pillion on my motorbike.

He smelled of treated cuttlefish and shrivelled red dates; told me he was the son of a dried sundries merchant and that they were made of money. He could give Ling Ko Mui the life a girl like her deserved. I went at him, but he had these lackeys with bad teeth and white singlets under unbuttoned shirts. They broke a rib of mine.

When I lay in hospital I thought about it like a carnival act. I'd reach into my throat, all the way in, and unearth this rib between my thumb and forefinger. I'd transfigure it into a bone-china rose and press it into her soft palm. She'd understand, she'd wrap her fingers around it and tell me that her heart had fallen on my side of the fence.

You're nothing, the merchant's son had said into my ear as his men held me back. You're just a loafer, sitting in the shade of a palm tree, playing your stupid songs to ten people in a pub. If I see you hanging around her again, you'll find the head of a pig on the front door of your father's house. My men are everywhere: if you speak with her, you'll find a parang in each of your kidneys the next morning—don't think I'm not up to this. He stamped my guitar to bits and spat into my face. Besides, you'll be doing yourself a favour, really—did you ever think for just one second that she would really go with a Malay boy?

That was when I knew I had to make it.

My guitar was my life. I stole money from a Chinese medicine hall and bought a new one, practised day in and day out. I stopped looking at girls. I stopped looking into the mirror. I grew calluses atop my calluses on my fingers. I made love to my guitar.

It took years, and I'm not going to pretend like it was easy, but I did it. I became famous. We had the adoration of schoolgirls and young women: Malay, Chinese and Indian. I never stopped looking for her face in the crowd, or imagining it, but deep down I knew he was right—she would never have been mine.

• • •

A constable was flagging Deddy Haikel's motorcycle down. Deddy Haikel's hair hung to his shoulders, blasé to the deterrent posters plastered all about town: *Males with Long Hair Will Be Attended To Last*. He wore motorcycle boots, a shirt with the top three buttons undone, and drainpipe jeans. These jeans were the sort that the police couldn't pass a Coke glass bottle through—the test that determined if your pants were too tight. If the Coke bottle couldn't come through your pant leg, you would have to remove your pants.

Deddy Haikel knew all the lyrics to the White Album, and John Lennon was his favourite Beatle because he'd heard through the grapevine—fancy Liverpool and Singapore neighbouring cities, not colonial affiliates—that when John Lennon met Yoko Ono, they went back to his place and made love all night. When John's wife, Cynthia, who had been out of town, walked through the door the next morning to see Yoko wrapped in her towel, all John said to Cynthia was—*Oh, hello.*

That is how a rock star should be, Deddy Haikel thought, as he lit a cig, as he picked chords on his guitar, as he thumbed the calluses on his fingers, as he rode a Malay girl, as the police were unable to pass the Coke bottle through his pant leg—*Oh, hello*.

Pants off, the Chinese constable told Deddy Haikel in Malay. Deddy Haikel shrugged his shoulders, grinned at the fellow. He wriggled out of them, with some effort because they were *that* tight. He hoped they wouldn't discard his jeans, that secretly back at HQ they would squeeze their fat Chinese calves into them, checking themselves out in the mirror, wishing they too could adopt these vistas of fashion, music, rebellion. Sighing as they holstered their batons, as they downed the dregs of their sock-kopi so as not to doze off on duty.

Deddy Haikel thought—a glowing, swollen thought that felt like the beginnings of a hard-on—as he passed his jeans amicably to the constable: in exactly twenty-four hours, I'll be on a stage. Paid to make girls scream. Don't you know who I am? Tomorrow I play the National Theatre. A sold-out show.

• • •

3,420 seats in the amphitheatre. 3,420 seats filled, and they all know the lyrics to every song, this makes him want to cry.

The back of the guitar against his pelvis, every twang amplified.

Malay girls, Chinese girls, Indian girls—all ages, and the same with men, but it is the girls he sees and the girls he hears, and they are screaming his name.

Mid-set someone throws a bullet-bra bustier onto the stage. As he leaves the microphone and bends to pick it up, he's thinking, John, hey John, I get it.

Deddy Haikel forgets to breathe because the song is his breath. He is thirsting and he is drinking in every yearning face in the crowd. He is not looking to a faraway point in the distance like his manager told him to, he is revelling in the specificity of each face, and he can see in their faces that they all want to touch him.

Twelve songs but it feels like it's just the first one even at the last. They think so too, they have banded together to demand *Encore, encore.*

Barbara shimmies down Bugis Street
And every sailor's head turns.
Feathers and a dress of midnight blue
Barbara's got an axe to burn.

He bows, his bandmates bow, they scream; he bows, his bandmates bow, they scream. The adrenaline crescendos, the area before his eyes explodes into tiny bright stars.

Peace.

• • •

They were walking to the carpark behind the National Theatre, equipment in tow, when a Rolls Royce pulled up in front of them. The backseat window rolled down.

Deddy Haikel, you did it.

Ling Ko Mui was smiling, shining. Long, finger-waved curls had replaced the schoolgirl bob, and her face was lightly made up. Only five years and now she was a woman.

This is my husband, Leong Heng.

It was the son of the dried goods merchant. In the backseat of the Rolls Royce, he looked perfectly civil. He smiled at Deddy Haikel, holding his hand up as a perfunctory greeting.

When I saw you on the poster I squealed, "I know him, he used to play at my father's pub!" I made Leong Heng get tickets right away. We had a marvellous time—it was a great performance.

Thank you.

It's a pity you stopped coming around to the pub though. I wanted to call you up at home but my father wouldn't give me your number. I'd thought maybe you lost interest in music.

No, that would never happen.

Well, then I guess our pub got too small for you.

It wasn't that either.

What was it, then?

My dear, you're not being very polite are you, Leong Heng interrupted, leaning over to put a hand on his wife's knee.

Look at me going on about the past. I don't mean to, Deddy Haikel. Congratulations again.

Thank you.

We should go, Leong Heng said. My heartiest congratulations to you.

He signalled to the driver, and the window began rolling up.

Goodbye, Ling Ko Mui said.

Goodbye, Deddy Haikel said, but the Rolls Royce had already pulled away.

• • •

The day they began tearing the National Theatre down in 1984—with its sharp rhombused frontal design, its amphitheatre, its crescent-shaped fountain—Deddy Haikel had his first heart attack.

Too much mutton, his first wife said. Too much cendol, his second wife chimed in. Too much kueh, his third wife added. This was his problem with having three wives. The rotational sex was good, but the three wives got along so well that they frequently rallied against him.

Sometimes he wondered how they could be so chummy—did he not inspire the surly beast of jealousy in his women? He tried to grunt and moan louder in his orgasms, so the other two wives who weren't on the master bedroom bed that night would hear. He hoped it kept them up at night, that they would try to outdo each other.

But they never did. They continued combing each other's hair, purchasing colourful faux silks when there was an offer at the market on each other's behalf, taking turns to bake sugee cookies for the brood, like sisters.

• • •

Wife Number One is signing in at the counter at Flamingo Valley for her visitor's pass. She's the fat one, the one who waddles when she walks, her ass expansive. She kisses his hands and they speak in Malay.

How are you, the doctor says you can come home soon? Still two more weeks?

Sayang, I'm still recovering from the bypass, look at me. He clutches his heart and pulls a face. Wife Number One frowns amusedly.

Five hundred dollars every week even after subsidy, you know.

Isn't that what I have seven children and three wives for?

He says this cheekily, with a roguish grin.

Wife Number One looks at him, exasperated, but it is a loving exasperation.

We need to save up for our retirement—you don't want to be a burden to the kids, do you?

Yeah okay, okay. It's not like I'm having a holiday here, you know. They poke all these needles into me three times a day, and the food is awful. I miss Khairah's beef rendang.

We'll get her to cook that on the day you return. I'll get the beef from the market.

Doctor says no more coconut milk and less red meat! Clogs up the heart.

How then?

Skim milk. Fish.

Poor Deddy. All your favourite things gone out the window.

She's near enough; he reaches out and squeezes her bottom gently. She pushes his hand in surprised outrage, turning to see if anyone's seen the act, but laughs.

Deddy, Deddy. She strokes his arm.

• • •

Deddy Haikel sits by Ling Ko Mui's bed. His is a shared ward of six but hers is a single.

Ling Ko Mui, do you believe in magic?

Ling Ko Mui looks at Deddy Haikel, shakes her head no.

How about fate, then?

She nods, very slowly. It's been awhile since questions such as these were asked of her, for a long time it'd been: How are you feeling today, Have you taken your medicine yet, Is it time to change those diapers?

She wants to speak, but language has been beyond her for so long. She shapes the words with her lips. *Whhh*. Nothing comes out.

Deddy Haikel is looking at her closely.

Fate is when you come from a different place from someone, but you keep seeing that person. Is that talking it down?

He scratches his head.

You know the way in your Chinese folktales, where the mortal spends a minute in Heaven and returns to Earth to find that thirty years have passed?

Ling Ko Mui is gesticulating, verging on speech.

A woman enters the ward, with her an unwilling child pulling on his own hands. Who's there? she demands.

Who're you? Deddy Haikel returns. The woman is affronted. This is my mother, the woman says, placing a hand on the side of Ling Ko Mui's bed.

Excuse me, Deddy Haikel says as he stands up, smoothing his johnnie shirt down and extending a hand, I'm an old friend of your mother's.

Really, the woman says skeptically. She doesn't take his hand. Ma, she says to Ling Ko Mui, who shows no interest in her nor the child. Call Ah Ma, the woman says to the child. Ah Ma, the child parrots. A nurse comes along, and the woman makes small talk with her, but as with long-stay nursing home talk, the talk is rarely substantive, prognoses seem at best a plateau, the only direction of progress often a slow careen towards certain death.

The nurse leaves and the woman eyes Deddy Haikel with suspicion again.

I used to perform in your grandfather's pub, he says.

The woman softens, looks at him now. My mother used to love talking about that place, she says, A pity I never got to see it for myself—demolished before I was born. She pauses. I'm sorry about earlier, she says. It's just—all the old people on this floor seem to have lost their marbles.

Don't worry about it. Deddy Haikel waves her apology away. I'm a short stay. Recovering from a heart bypass. Still got my marbles, for now at least.

She smiles at him.

Where's your father? Deddy Haikel asks, suddenly.

He passed away from a stroke several years ago, the woman says.

I'm sorry to hear that.

It's just so difficult having to deal with this again, the woman says, shutting her eyes briefly. I'm glad he's not here to see this, though—if you knew them, you must have known how much he doted on her.

Deddy Haikel strains to smile. The woman smiles back.

What did you play back then?

It was the 60s, sayang. Everyone played rock 'n' roll. A touch of Pop Yé-yé.

• • •

It smarts when he thinks about it later that night, the life Ling Ko Mui shared with the son of the dried goods merchant.

Five decades, half a century. He tosses in bed, dreams of an eighteen-year-old girl in a white skirt, eating nasi kandar with both hands.

Deddy Haikel sneaks into Ling Ko Mui's single ward before dawn. When she opens her eyes about an hour later, there he sits. It startles her, but she's always had a strong heart.

Ling Ko Mui, remember when I brought you to eat goreng pisang? You loved it. Remember when I took you to eat nasi kandar? You asked me why Malay chilli was sweet.

She's shrinking away from him in a sleepy stupor, but already there's the taste of deep-fried bananas, kampung chicken and yellow rice in her mouth.

Do you remember, when you brought me to eat dough fritters and soybean milk, and I was like, Why the hell would you guys dip the fritters into the soybean milk, wouldn't it lose its crisp? You laughed at that. Remember? Or when I told you I'd have to pray ten times a day because you were taking me to eat food that wasn't halal? How when I tried to kiss you later, you said "But I'm not halal", and then you closed your eyes and leaned in anyway?

Ling Ko Mui looks at Deddy Haikel's hand. She opens her mouth. The words don't come out, but she's nodding, this time with confidence. She's smiling. She reaches out for his hand. Before he gives it to her, he draws the peach curtains apart, throws the windows open. He sits by her bed, gives her his hand. He doesn't ask more, doesn't nudge her to speak, doesn't venture to ascertain what it is she remembers. They remain like this till the sun comes up. He has an eye on the clock. He removes his hand from hers at 7.15am, before the breakfast trolley comes around to the single wards.

As he moves away to the door, he hears a rustle of bedclothes. He turns, and she is reaching out for him, the way a child might.

He walks over to her bed, kisses a prominent vein on the left side of her forehead. His faulty heart thuds from acting on impulse. He leaves briskly, just missing the breakfast trolley on its rounds as it turns the corner on the other end of the corridor.

• • •

She begins responding to her name, but only if the doctors and nurses say it in full with an exclamation—*Ling Ko Mui!*—not if they call her Mrs Tan, or Madam Ling, or Auntie, Asian assumptions of preferred deference.

She's stopped needing her bedpan. They bring her for physiotherapy sessions now. Atrophy is easy, effortless; but when you have something to live for—even if you're not sure what it is—the body fights back.

They call her daughter, informing her of these improvements. Ling Ko Mui's daughter arrives to witness the changes for herself, but is still ignored by her mother, who simply stares straight ahead in her daughter's presence. She returns home and thinks: what a waste of time. She isn't sure if there's a difference between a bedridden dementia patient and a more active dementia patient.

Ling Ko Mui still can't speak, but her mouth contorts itself around language as she remembers it. They see the marked change in her, the younger nurses aren't so hardened as to let this pass. They try to encourage her.

They ask her: What do you remember?

Ling Ko Mui remembers five stars and a moon.

But the five stars are a building's pointed façade, and the moon is crescent, with jets of water shooting out of it. She draws this for the nurses, who are puzzled.

She's walking towards it, it's a futuristic brick-and-brown building and as she passes the threshold the crescent moon-like fountain dies down. She files past the box office, enters a sprawling hall of 3,420 seats, takes her place. She looks up to the cantilevered roof. When she looks back down all the seats are filled, Deddy Haikel and his band are on stage, and the music is inside her.

Deddy Haikel, she writes on the piece of paper shakily, Deddy Haikel.

It is lunchtime, and the nurses wheel her to him. She sits with him in the halal section of the cafeteria. She looks up into his face, she touches his cheek from time to time, his forehead, as if anointing him.

He smiles, first with his lips pressed together, then breaking out into a crinkle-eyed grin. He picks up his guitar, propping it on his knee.

And she begins singing with him, in perfect time, the lyrics word for word.

Barbara shimmies down Bugis Street
And every sailor's head turns.
Feathers and a dress of midnight blue
Barbara's got an axe to burn.

• • •

The nurses show Deddy Haikel the paper where Ling Ko Mui has sketched the diamonds and the crescent. They want to know if he knows what it is. They have romanticised it as some cosmic hieroglyph.

It's the National Theatre, Deddy Haikel says decidedly.

What's that?

Deddy Haikel shakes his head.

Another dead national monument. Do you know they had a-dollar-a-song campaign for it on the radio? You called in and paid a dollar and the DJ dedicated a song to you, and that dollar went to the building fund.

That sounds fun, one of the nurses says.

Fun? It was pride. We were a new nation. Everyone buys their firstborn the best clothes. Rich businessmen made phone calls arranging for direct contributions, trishaw riders called in to the radio with their day's savings earned through backbreaking work, and went hungry after. These days, they do whatever they want. It's still your money they're using, except they don't remind you of the fact any more, and you don't get a tune out of it. They don't want it to get personal.

What happened to it?

Twenty-three years was what it was worth, demolished to make way for part of the Central Expressway underground tunnel.

The tunnel? I thought this was what happened with the National Library on Stamford Road.

Well, it would seem then that we're always one tunnel short, wouldn't you say?

• • •

Ling Ko Mui's talking, pissing and shitting of her own conscious accord, asking the nurses and doctors plucky little questions. Her sudden recovery is a miracle, that much is agreed upon. The doctors shake their head at the mysteries of neurobiology.

She and Deddy Haikel sit in the herb garden in the sunshine.

So girl, let me ask you something: what's going to happen to you when I'm gone?

I'll tell my parents I want to be with you. They can't stop me.

He starts in his seat. He wants to say, *Baby, look at me. Look at you*, but he can't bring himself to do it. He's waited half a lifetime for this.

And, and if they do?

Then we elope.

What about my bandmates?

They'll come with us. I'll be your agent.

She has an impish look in her eyes.

There's something I've been meaning to ask you. What about Leong Heng?

Who?

The son of the dried goods merchant.

What are you talking about?

Sorry, I—nothing.

Who's that?

It's nothing, I just—there are so many people out there who could provide better for you. I don't have much to offer you.

Look into my eyes, Deddy Haikel: you have nothing to worry about.

Deddy Haikel will leave in four days. Every night he dreams of the eighteen-year-old girl, and every morning he wakes to be with her. They have their meals together, they talk about music, he plays songs for her. She talks about her parents, she talks about being with him. She doesn't question why they're surrounded by the elderly and infirm, the doctors and nurses in uniform, nor where they are.

At night Deddy Haikel thinks to himself, he's setting things up for heartbreak, but what else can he do? He never thought this would happen to him at seventy. He pictures his girl segueing back into silence and incontinence upon his departure. He's done this to her, it is done.

Tomorrow he will tell her.

• • •

She won't have anything to do with it. Her puzzlement is giving over to angry tears.

Ling Ko Mui, listen to me. Look at my face—I'm an old man. We've already lived our entire lives out.

She's jammed her knobbly hands over her ears, she's sobbing inconsolably like a young girl.

I can't be with you now. I have children, wives; a family.

She turns to him hotly, tears and loathing in her eyes, hands still over her ears, says in a low tone: *I'll never let another Malay boy break my heart.*

Ling Ko Mui, you don't understand.

He tries to come over to her, places his hands on her upturned elbows, says, I could come visit you, but she shrugs him off.

Get out, she hisses, rocking back and forth on the nursing home bed, *get out.*

• • •

At Flamingo Valley, Ling Ko Mui's daughter is speaking to the doctor, distraught. She doesn't understand why her mother has recovered her faculties but not her memory of her family. She'd tried explaining to her mother—for the umpteenth time—who she was, but all Ling Ko Mui muttered was some gibberish, over and over. *De-de-hi-ke, de-de-hi-ke.*

The nurses know who Ling Ko Mui is asking for, but they also know he checked out this morning, and what would be the point of attempting to explain to the daughter?

In a flat in Tampines, Deddy Haikel is home. Khairah's cooked beef rendang, Azzizah's made lontong, Fathiah, who can't cook, has prepared sirap bandung in a jug. Skim milk in all three cases, they hasten to impress upon him. The children gripe that it doesn't taste the same, not as lemak, but they're happy to have their old man back.

Deddy Haikel's heart murmurs, skips beats. He picks up his guitar absently, strums and sings. He imagines reaching into his chest cavity, disentangling heartstrings, affixing them on his guitar, like pro tennis racquets strung with Taranaki cow guts. What would that sound like? He tugs at a chord. He's thinking of writing lyrics and melodies again. Songs for an eighteen-year-old girl.

Carousel & Fort

IT WAS MY director's directive, the curator said before she'd even settled herself into the wicker chair, looking at the slightly smug, bemused—or so it seemed, to her—expression on the artist's face. She folded her hands tightly in her lap, over the skirt that grazed her knee. She'd changed out of permutations and combinations of five outfits before deciding on this, a decision she regretted right before entering the cab. As it had pulled up, she saw her reflection in the tinted windowpane and thought: I look like I'm attending a state funeral.

The artist held his hands up, smiling and shrugging disarmingly. His hair had begun to grey, a touch that lent credibility to his appearance, she thought. He was in a rumpled grey t-shirt and this made her feel even more foolish as she sucked in her stomach, corseted as it was by the severe-looking pencil skirt.

You've gotten so—he ran his fingers through his hair—corporate. He smiled and leaned back. They were in the outdoor smoking area of a sidewalk café, a neutral space almost exactly in between his studio and the museum at which she worked.

She stirred the stick of honey into her coffee, looking at him, resolutely deadpan. She said: We leave it to the artists to be bohemian.

He leaned forward abruptly—Tell me, do you still paint?

No, she said, quiet but furious. Never.

They both picked up their coffee cups and took a drink. As she settled hers back down onto the saucer, she managed to say, Besides—as evidenced by your success—painting is dead. She took out a leather-bound notebook and a pen. Now, shall we?

He steepled his fingers agreeably.

When you developed *Carousel*, the work where the cross-sectionally halved carcasses of two horses are suspended and chained on opposing ends of a metal rod to a fulcrum and dragged across the floor for the full duration of the exhibition, what was your process; what were you thinking of?

You.

Excuse me?

I was thinking of you.

Why are you making this harder than it has to be?

Suddenly, she felt very, very tired. The buzzing edge that had made her snappy to her subordinates, curt to her superiors, and unable to get a decent night's rest for the whole week had expired. She wanted to go home. Perhaps she could get a medical certificate for the rest of the week. Perhaps she would not be able to curate this exhibition; it would really only be one more addition to the long line of things he had ruined for her. Perhaps she should apply to a higher position in the new private museum that would be opening at the end of the year, the one that was rumoured to be financed by an oil sheikh. It was about time to make a career move anyway.

I'm not trying to make things difficult for you. I'm talking to you as a human being, as an artist, coarse as they come. I tell you the base instinct, you turn it to gold. It's your job to make my work sound polished. Besides, c'mon, it's not at all like I was thinking of you throughout my practice. *Carousel* was a very early work.

She looked at him. He looked at her. She ordered one more flat white. She dislodged the clasp of her clutch and brought out a pack of menthols, then lit up and exhaled.

He said: What happened to the Sampoernas?

They were too cloying.

He said: Okay, okay. When I made *Carousel*, what I was thinking of was this: the inevitable, cyclical failure of relationships. How bloody it is. How tiring it is. How persistent we—the universal plural that is—are. The carcasses are spun across the gallery floor till the meat gets worn down to the bone. They are both in pursuit of one another but they will always be the same distance apart. The circular spread of blood across the floor, the carcass as a blunt, honest apparatus of painting. To paint in blood with a stump of flesh, over blood that has dried over itself. It never ends till we're bled dry. It's a macabre, visceral celebration of failure and persistence, the failed persistence or the persistent failure of love if you like, in all its guts and glory.

She did not look up from her notebook as her pen flew across the page.

She said: People go to see *Carousel*, and they throw up.

Yes, and I love that—I love it when there is a physiological reaction to my work. I find it so flattering. It seems something dramatic always tends to happen with my larger works. It is pain, it is discomfiture, it is nausea. But isn't that true to life, to the way things end?

Do you enjoy causing hurt? She looked up briefly. Is the pain, discomfiture and nausea on your agenda, as an artist?

He seemed to laugh and frown at the same time. I don't aspire to that, no. It isn't foremost in my mind. They are reactionary by-products that I feel attest to the physical and emotional brutality of my work, but it isn't something I actively seek out in my process—how should I pain my viewer?—the process is much purer, in that it is, I admit, self-absorbed.

You admit to being self-absorbed?

I admit to my process being self-absorbed. But if you must, yes—I admit to being self-absorbed, as should every good artist.

Let us talk about your recent work *Fort*, the one that has everyone riled up. You've constructed a simple sangar breastwork with pebbles you picked in Iran, where the sacks encasing the pebbles are the burqas of Iranian women you met and offered money to.

I'm sure you've heard about this already, but it's too important to not make certain—it's not an urban legend—I offered them money for the very burqa on their body.

Could you elaborate on the motivation behind that?

I wanted to know at what price one can be coerced into disavowing one's beliefs, one's modesty, one's dignity.

And they would walk home naked?

Well, they would usually try to run. In their undergarments. Not all of them wore undergarments, though. I must say however that the project is fatally weaker than it should have been—for the moment they turned around to leave, I would stop them and hand them a fresh burqa, so they wouldn't be shamed.

How does it weaken the project? It makes you less despicable. Gallant, almost.

Precisely. Gallantry isn't strength, it's a deference to restraint. Their shame, my brutality, would have raised the conceptual price on the head of a project like this. It's like the photojournalist who waited for the vulture to close in on the starving Sudanese child before he pressed the shutter and left it there.

Only this time you were both the vulture and the photojournalist.

Yes. But—don't look at me like that, you're a curator, we're in this contemporary hot soup together—it is a leap of faith to engender the opposite of a leap of faith. I only wanted to push something as far as it could logically go. The moment she strips off her burqa for me for a certain sum of money—US dollars, I might add—I've proven my point, and I can't bear to shame her further.

Why did you want to make this project? You've never been interested in religion in your practice. And I hear you've received the requisite death threats from the Islamic fundamentalists who've gotten wind.

Do you really want to know?

What do you mean?

Yes, or no.

All right.

Is that a yes?

She rolled her eyes. Yes.

I'd like to keep this off the record, but I was in love with an Iranian reporter at that time. She, too, loved me, but she said we could never be together because I wasn't Muslim. Strict atheist though I was and am, I did actually love her enough to consider converting to Islam, but I thought about it long and hard and I couldn't do it because it meant that she didn't love me enough to see past something categorical. If I'd converted to Islam, Allah would have won, and she would always love him more than me.

You're crazy.

I wanted to make a work that would make her rethink her assumptions and beliefs. I wanted it to be a slap in the face to her. At the same time, I wanted the slap to be charming and clever and outlandish, I wanted her to love me for the sting it left on her cheek. And so I went around Iran, playing the devil propositioning these local women, one pocket stuffed full of dollar bills, the other laden with the pebbles I was collecting by hand. My gait was lopsided. Sometimes I felt like Virginia Woolf packing her pockets with stones to weigh her body down. I felt so burdened, so drained. I felt like I was walking into the River Ouse, I felt like I was drowning in the dunes of the Dasht-e Kavir.

How very touching, she said with a slight sneer that she'd calibrated so it wouldn't seem vicious. She stubbed out her cigarette. Well—did it work?

She was the one who told the Basji fundamentalists about me.

Oh my god—I'm sorry to hear that.

I'm not.

Why?

In a way, it was then I knew how much she loved me.

The curator slapped her notebook down onto the table and laughed. She threw her head back. Her laughter was sincere. You're really—you're really something, aren't you? Why didn't you tell this story to the press, though? They would've lapped it up. It's feature film-worthy.

Because it's between me and her. It's far more romantic this way. Everyone else's got their knickers in a twist because of the politics and the religion, but really, for us, it's just a love story. It's so romantic it would kill my name as an artist.

For a moment she desperately wanted him back. Then as quickly as it came over her, it passed. She was glad that a substantial heft of time had elapsed and that the sensation had passed without undue thought. She felt surer of herself now.

You're such a ladies' man.

They both laughed.

I do love my women, he said.

I note the plural tense, she said lightly. But seriously: is every work of yours about a woman? Doesn't that emasculate you in a way?

Not every work of mine is about a woman. But even if it were so, I wouldn't be afraid of that emasculation. That's how much I love women. I don't pretend that my existence would be complete without them. I don't mind if my work springs from their rib.

Would you say, then, that when you enter into a relationship, you're looking to make art out of it?

God, no.

She lit up again. She offered him the pack, and he took a stick. She extended her lighter towards him; he cupped his hand around hers as the flame trembled in the breeze.

• • •

How long does it take for an artist to make a career? How long does it take for an artist to give up?

They'd met at the scholarship ceremony, more than two decades ago. He'd noticed her slim legs onstage as she shook hands with the minister, the shy bow and smile she gave. His girlfriend was with him at the ceremony, but when she went to the bathroom, he went up to the girl with the legs and said, Glasgow? Goldsmiths? SVA? RCA?

She looked a little taken aback, even as she stepped aside from her parents and said, Glasgow.

I'll be there too, he said, I'll look out for you.

In Glasgow, they'd moved in together within the first month. Six months into the relationship, he told her about his extant girlfriend back home. She threw a glass ashtray at him and walked out the door, but came back crying that very night. He held her tight and promised to end it, but when the girlfriend came to Glasgow for Christmas, he squired the girl with the legs off to live in a dorm for the two weeks, packing off all her clothes and trinkets and the photo booth strips of them into a cardboard box that he stashed in his campus locker. For the whole of that year and the next, he continued seeing both girls simultaneously.

She was wearing his oversized, threadbare Flaming Lips t-shirt and he could see her thong under it as he came through the door. When they first got together, she would wear sweaters and capris at home, but as the year went by, he noticed her changing for him. He knew she found thongs uncomfortable but he'd told her how good it made him feel to see her in one. He'd in fact just returned from a quick liaison with the foundation year life-drawing model in the sculpting studio in the west wing on campus. The model was a redhead and when he'd charcoaled in her pubic hair the lack of colour had seemed such a shame.

Where were you? she'd asked, smiling at him as he walked towards her. There was white paint on her nose and he flicked it off tenderly.

I was playing with clay—I'm considering changing my major.

Did you know that Dalí was afraid of women with body hair?

That's really funny.

They moved to her easel, by the window.

Y'know, you're really good, he said, nuzzling her behind the ear.

Only technically, she said. I don't have the flair. I know it. But you, she turned to face him, You're really—you're really something, aren't you?

• • •

On the night of the artist's opening at the museum, the curator was in a midnight blue dress that showed off her figure. The artist was in a black blazer over a rumpled grey t-shirt. The curator noticed that he'd dyed his grey hairs black when they air-kissed in greeting. The curator was speaking with a pair of collectors. The artist was listening to the director's institutional spiel. He was flipping through the exhibition catalogue, noticing—and smiling at—the curator's choice of words: *faith-seeking brutality, an iconoclast-saviour complex, satyriasis, despair, extravagant syntax, "Art is a lie that makes us realise truth"*. She'd asked him to vet the curatorial essay, but he'd laughed and said, Leave me dazzled.

A fat man in pinstripes was shaking his hand; the director was making introductions. The viewing public was mostly standing around *Carousel* in the main gallery, silent, whilst his smaller-scale works lay littered and lonely in the annexes like afterthoughts. A fair smattering of people surrounded *Fort* too, in the antechamber, these ones talking animatedly. A waiter came by with canapés. There was a prawn and mango mousse concoction on a porcelain spoon. The artist picked that, and having consumed it, wondered what he was to do with the spoon. He held on to it, feeling a little silly.

At around 9pm, a car bomb went off on the front lawn of the museum. Women in high heels were screaming. A limb, blown off, hung below a painting. Guests lay crushed dead by pillars of the museum, whose structure was a reclaimed art-deco missionary boys' school. The artist, hit by shrapnel in the back of the head, died almost instantly.

Most of the gallery was falling to rubble. The burqa-sacks of *Fort* were burning, leaving the pebbles behind, innocuous, cleansed, a trial by fire. *Carousel* had not been felled; it stood like the ruins of an old fairground. The suspension cable was damaged and the halved carcasses were no longer on either ends of the metal pole—they were almost touching one another, and they were on fire. The circumference of blood they had drawn across the floor was lightened with a layer of dust and strewn with rubble.

The curator, too, was not hurt; the impact had merely thrown her to the ground. She found herself entirely mesmerised by *Carousel*. She could not bring herself to move to safety. She had to keep watching. The electrical wiring of the gallery had blown, the lights were out, but the two flaming carcasses were still spinning on principles of physics. One was almost catching up with the other now. The smell of charred meat—whether it was the horses or the guests of the opening—was beginning to perfume the air. With each round, the carcasses were slowing down unevenly on their metal suspension cord. They dragged on the ground sluggishly, roasting from the neck up, bleeding from the flank down, leaving a textured trail of red and rubble in their wake.

Pawn

DELIA WAS THE sort of woman you took one look at and instantly knew she'd never once been touched by a man. Perhaps it was in her gait, the slight, awkward twitch of her philtrum before she smiled, or the exact angle at which she tucked her purse under her arm as she headed out for lunch each day. She smelled lightly of mothballs, though there were no mothballs in her wardrobe.

Still, it puzzled her that she was alone. She knew she wasn't beautiful, but she looked around her, and there were so many men who were ugly, too. It seemed clear enough to her that they deserved each other. Yet these men only had eyes for the pretty women in the office building, holding open elevator doors, loaning umbrellas, offering up gifts of uninitiated teh ping. These pretty women, with their long hair and painted nails, accepted these little putative alms with coquettish smiles, but behind the backs of these ugly men, in the company of the other women—that is, the ugly women—they ragged these ugly men—*as if I would ever go out with somebody like that.* The particular mark of ugliness of the man would be enumerated—a face like a bullfrog, body odour, a lardy bottom paired with tight, outmoded trousers.

Then they would all be expected to laugh in feminine camaraderie, though of course these pretty women knew they were being unnecessarily cruel—to the ugly men yes, but more so, and with crystal clarity, it was a jibe at the ugly women, who could not solicit the attention of even these ugly men: the lowest of low-hanging fruit. You could see this glint of triumph manifest in the eyes of the pretty women as they filed out of the pantry, toting their mugs, the prettiest women with the brightest mugs.

Delia had a dull mug, a free gift from one of their client's events. She'd been tempted once by a ceramic magenta mug with a printed black lace motif. She bought it furtively, only to return home to realise she'd left it on the public bus. After that, she knew that even these small, futile gestures performed in the hopes of self-comfort were grating on the nerves of a higher power.

She stopped trying. She once collected dresses one size too small, that she could marginally squeeze into, the zip intermittently nipping her skin. She once bought mineral make-up in hues and iridescences she was unsure of. She held her tummy in and stood before the mirror, tossing her hair half-heartedly, but she had plump sloping shoulders and no collarbones. She could never step out of her room, much less her house. To don a pretty dress, to bedaub shimmery eye shadow, was to not know her place. The pretty women would call her bluff, she would be a laughingstock.

• • •

There was an economical kiosk tucked away in a corner of their office tower on the ground floor, where variants of tea and coffee and pre-packed boxes of limp bee hoon and nasi lemak could be bought cheaply.

Whilst the pretty women often trotted off to the salad bars and the gourmet sandwich and wrap cafés, Delia and her rank would make sojourns to kiosks such as these. It wasn't that the pretty women earned more, it was just that they had better reasons to eat better, to see and be seen. It was like the income disparity gap—the rich became richer, the poor became poorer.

Since Delia started work in this building four years ago, the kiosk she frequented most often had been manned by a testy middle-aged woman, who handed back her change with oily hands. Today though, as Delia approached the counter, in place of said woman was a beautiful boy in a dirty blue singlet. She cleared her throat, quite suddenly thick and scratchy.

Bee hoon, please, plus a chicken drumstick. No no, drumstick, not wing. *Drumstick.*

She pointed at the cut of meat from the other side of the display glass.

Sorry, he said in accented Mandarin, putting a hand to his head in an apologetic salute.

Delia found herself searching for something to say. You're new here, she said in Mandarin as she pressed the coins and notes into his outstretched hand.

Yes.

Are you from China?

Yes, Harbin.

I hear its cold there.

Oh yes. Our winter winds blow from Siberia.

Is that why your cheeks are so rosy?

He looked at her, amused and perplexed. He reached up to

touch his cheek, leaving a grease mark. He couldn't have been more than twenty.

Someone appeared in line behind her, ordering a kopi O.

She took her styrofoam-packed lunch in its thin coral-pink plastic bag in both hands and moved on.

• • •

I was just thinking, you might not have been shown around Singapore. Only tourists go sightseeing, right? And, I've noticed, you work weekends too. I was wondering, perhaps if we could go for supper? I know a really good place with chilli crab—it's a famous Singaporean dish—just around the corner.

That's really nice of you, but oh, I don't know.

Why not?

Maybe I should head home and have a shower and change into something nicer?

No, don't worry about it. Look, I'll buy you a new shirt you can pull over right now, how about that?

Now he's in a t-shirt from Bossini, the ones that say I ♥ SG, an incredibly bad rip-off of Milton Glaser's iconic I ♥ NY, the ratty singlet a sour potpourri of testosterone and no-minimum-wage labour in his bag. And there she is, Delia, finding herself peeling crab for him.

He is sucking on the claws, making these little guzzling sounds, popping the proffered succulent white flesh into his mouth. She is watching his plump red lips. She breaks off a mantou and mops up some gravy with the doughy interior, handing it to him.

Do you eat crab in Harbin?

When we catch it ourselves. We fish for carp and crab by the creek. It's too expensive to eat it in restaurants. He realises what he's said and he looks at her sheepishly.

Oh, don't worry about it, she says, realising that she hasn't eaten anything, absentmindedly chewing on some plain bit of the other half of the fried mantou, and then she adds a qualifier: As long as you're enjoying yourself.

He puts down the vermillion crab claw and looks at her seriously, Yes, I am, I am.

She pays and they leave the eatery. She feels exultant walking beside him. She catches herself staring at the vein trailing his forearm, his work-roughened hands. At the bus stop, she ensures he knows which bus to take, east-bound to his cheap shared dormitory apartment. Her bus is pulling into the bus bay. She bids him goodbye.

Is there anything I can do for you? His face is earnest.

Now that the question is out in the open, it catches her by such surprise.

She's lifted a foot, about to board the bus, she hovers mid-step. She opens and shuts her mouth. He sees from her face that there's something he can do for her but that she doesn't yet know how to say it, and he springs from the bus stop bench and boards the bus with her, pulling her in, along. The doors swing shut.

Lei, she says his name breathlessly, as if he's crossed an ocean for her, and perhaps he has. Dismay, mixed with obvious pleasure.

What is it? he asks, face warm and open and genuine. For a

split second, Delia catches herself thinking, It was just one crab. Just one crab and now you're wagging your tail at me, rolling over. She thinks it in a grateful, simpering way, as if she might like to cry.

It was just—I was wondering if you might walk me home.

Delia has never been walked home ever, and she almost says this, pulling back at the last moment: There've been a couple of armed robberies in my estate lately, you see.

That's all?

It sounds suddenly, precariously, like a scoff, but then he's smiling that wide-open smile again, saying, *Of course* I can do that. *Of course* I can walk you home.

The three hundred metres from the bus stop to her block of flats have never been dearer. Lei gets the elevator for her, asks after her floor level, presses eight. He walks her all the way to her gate, where the unwieldy potted plants—with their eggshells in the soil and the red ribbons tied to their branches—and her mother's pink plastic sandals, grimy and splitting apart, embarrass her.

But she realises he is completely unperturbed, looking at her as a child might.

Thank you, she says.

No problem.

Goodnight.

Goodnight—will you buy lunch from me tomorrow?

Yes.

You've been buying the same thing from me for a whole week now. Don't—it's not so healthy to eat that every day, is it?

Get some soup instead.

She smiles and takes out her keys, glancing at her watch.

Gosh, it's past midnight. How are you going to get back? There'll be no more buses, and taxis will be carrying a surcharge. Here—she passes him twenty dollars—Take this.

I can walk, he says, but already he is reaching out to accept the two red and beige notes.

• • •

Delia's in a dress, one size too small. The form of her love handles is visible from the back, dribbling over the elastic band of her underwear. She has bronzed her eyelids. She is wearing mascara, already slightly smudged though it is only lunchtime.

Lei sees Delia in her dress, the make-up. The moment he does, he knows he's won. A small smile plays out inside his lips, around the corners of his mouth. There's a space on either side of our lower lips, under the corners of our mouths, where our canine teeth would have been; traces of things we've lost through the course of evolution. Lei knows he's won, and Delia doesn't even know this is a game.

The pretty women had swallowed their surprise at Delia's appearance—not all of it, just enough to remain polite. *Delia, you look so different!* Delia couldn't have cared less. She kept her eye on the clock on the wall, filing her reports diligently, sitting up straighter.

Bee hoon, please—

And a drumstick?

Yes.

She's smiling at him. She checks to see his boss isn't around: Dinner tonight?

• • •

Lei comes home to his dorm mates crowded around the floor of their cramped room, lights turned off but for the glow from his brand-new 15-inch laptop and the intermittent bluc light of his mobile internet stick. They have hiked the volume all the way up and the moaning from the low-fidelity AV is sharp as broken glass. Some of his dorm mates have their cocks in hand, others are squatting around, staring intently at the screen.

Our man, Lei, one of them says.

Lei comes around, sees the two Japanese girls onscreen, slim but with large, fake breasts, the man penetrating them in turn, his penis huge and hairless. The girls are moaning, out of sync with one another, and one of them is squeezing her breasts together with her small hands.

Shit. Look at these Japs. If I ever got my hands on one—

I told you guys not to touch my stuff without asking me, Lei says.

So selfish, Lei.

Don't you want to share your goods with your comrades, Lei?

Lei, can your woman buy me a handphone too?

Suck my cock, Lei says.

At least I didn't say laptop. Give me your handphone and tell her you lost yours and need a new one.

I said—suck my cock.

Really?

Lei looks at his dorm mate in disgust. Another chimes in: Does she suck your cock, Lei?

If I wanted her to.

Why wouldn't you want her to?

A fourth: I've seen her. She looks like a yak.

She's not that bad, Lei says defensively.

Ooh, Lei. Do you care for her?

Howls of laughter all around, the slapping of thighs. The Japanese ménage a trois is coming to a climax, together, one of the women masturbating whilst watching the other woman get fucked.

Our Lei here is a precious little gigolo, isn't he?

Lei bends over and snaps the laptop screen shut. Hey motherfucker, one of his dorm mates says, gesturing with his left hand to the erect penis in his right. Give it here, pussy.

Lei thinks about putting a fist in the face of his countryman. He picks up the laptop with one hand, turns, but there's nowhere for him to walk off to, no door to lock unless it is the toilet. He looks around—the eight of them, the four bunk beds, the clothes laid out to dry on the frames and stepladder rungs of their bunk beds, the electric stove and the rice cooker. Their polyester duffel bags under the bed, most still with baggage tags on, denoting their city airport codes: HRB, DLU, PVG, JJN.

Lei eases up. He puts his laptop down, reopens the screen, sits down. His dorm mates crowd around him. He takes the porn from the top. When it resumes, amidst the jerking hands and guttural grunts of his compatriots—augmented with a slap on the back, a friendly grab at his crotch, fraternal encouragement to get into it—Lei feels like he is home, away from home.

• • •

Delia and her parents are watching the 9pm Chinese drama serial on the box telly in the living room. The show ends and the credits roll. Delia's parents agreed this morning that they would bring it up tonight, to come right out and say it after three months of unspoken oscillation between disgruntlement and concern.

Ling, why have you cut down our allowances?

Delia keeps her eyes glued to the screen.

Are… are things okay at the office?

Things are a bit slow.

Pay cut?

Delia nods. Her parents exchange glances and her father swallows.

Ling, don't worry, her mother says gently, have a job very good already.

Delia nods vacantly, excuses herself from the worn PVC sofa, where the parts accommodating bottoms and thighs are cracked through, peeling like ripe fruit. She goes to her room, closes the door. Outside, scored by the 9pm Chinese theme song, her parents look at each other, worried they have upset their daughter. Delia's mother begins peeling an orange. Delia's father turns on the radio, tuned to the Chinese oldies.

In her room, on the bed she's had since she was fourteen, Delia lies on her back, next to the stuffed toys that still share her bed. She picks up her phone, begins typing a message to a contact she has saved as 宝贝. *Baby*, like they always said on the radio, and now she has one to call her own.

Baby I miss you, she types in Chinese characters.

Five minutes later, the reply, Me too.

What are you doing?

Thinking of you.

Before that?

Still thinking of you.

Before before that?

Doing my laundry.

Can't wait to see you tomorrow after work.

Me too. Rest early, sweet dreams.

Delia's mother knocks on the door. Ling? I cut some oranges.

Delia doesn't reply, and the knocking continues, tentatively.

Leave it outside, Ma. I'll eat later.

• • •

It's Christmas and she's watching him unwrap his presents. He'd told her previously about the beautiful ice sculptures they have in Harbin every year in January, and she'd said, You must take me there one day, maybe next year? They're sitting in a café in a touristy part of town, near a canal that is called a river, plied by repurposed bumboats chockfull of Caucasian and Japanese tourists.

He holds the gifts up, a crisp long-sleeved shirt and smart

pants. He's been waiting for an excuse for a while now, an exit strategy. What's this, he demands.

I thought you'd look handsome in them.

Are you embarrassed to be seen with me? Because I don't work in an office? Is this what this is?

No, no, Lei, it's nothing like that. I just thought—

Well, don't think I'm so happy to be seen with you either. Even the girl who cleans the toilet is better-looking than you.

What girl?

She's from Malaysia. She cleans the toilet in our building. Haven't you seen her around? Slim and fair, with a heart-shaped face.

Lei—

What.

Lei—

He stands up. She's started crying.

What do you want, Lei? I can go get it. I only bought you these because I'd gotten you everything else already—the phone, laptop, mp3 player—I thought it'd be fun, I just thought you would look handsome, really, that's all.

I've had enough of your face.

Lei, don't you love me? You said you loved me.

He doesn't even bother to feed his lines properly, just makes to go. She catches his wrist.

Don't go. I'll—I'll pay you to stay.

This he did not expect. He'd expected to be called a cad, to have been reviled. Angry tears, demands for the gifted items to be returned. But this, this was a whole new level.

He pauses, and she holds her breath—maybe this was all an awful mistake, he would say, What kind of question is that, baby, what do you take my affection for?—he's opening his mouth now, and he says:

How much?

• • •

He's in the shirt and pants she got him for Christmas, and a pair of shiny leather brogues. They're strolling down Robertson Quay, and she's looking up at him adoringly. He looks so handsome, really, he does.

The women they stroll past stare a split second too long at the unlikely couple. It isn't so uncommon for a man here to have a girlfriend out of his league, but you seldom saw an ugly woman with a man much too handsome for her. With a good job too, by the looks of the brogues and the branded leather briefcase.

Whether they are single, or with partners in tow, there's an indignant, bitter taste rising from the backs of their throats, because what she has is one in a million—he must truly see past the physical hull of her, right into her. This must be love, then.

And in that shining moment as the lips of these women curl, even if it is to turn to their partners to say, Would you still love me if I looked like *that*?, the facts of the matter are no longer important. The logical direction of the food chain, obvious only a moment ago, is suspect. It's a fact, not a question: the question is not her love for him, his lack of love for her, if there is love, or even what love is; the fact is that love is out of the question. Only power is left and the turning table is, in passing, suspended—and for now, with precipitant clarity, he is ancillary, and she is queen. As the women bat their eyes in contemptuous envy, injudiciously affronted by the anomaly of the pair, Lei is supplanted, and Delia wins.

The King of Caldecott Hill

HE DOESN'T LOOK exactly the way he does on the telly, and it surprises her that this surprises her, because, obviously, showbiz *is* showbiz, and she's twenty-one; she's come of age, she knows better.

In a way, he has always been the leading male presence in her life. After her father left, her mother never stayed with one man for more than two years a pop, but the Channel 8 Chinese drama serials were always on at 7pm and 9pm. With his popularity, she could count on him to be on every other new show, it was a matter of two months at most—the TV station works on a 30-episode basis, generally. He's barely gone to seed at all though he's verging on fifty now.

The King of Caldecott Hill clicks his fingers at her. She's been idling. She can't move, she's seven again, watching him on the telly when her mother waltzes into the living room with a new man, just as the then fresh-faced King of Caldecott Hill announces to the baddie with the awful perm—yes, the same unfortunate dude who always plays the baddie—"我就以这十块钱赢你这家赌场!" [1] He's in a white shirt with a silver bowtie and a matching cummerbund. Her mother says, Say hi to Uncle, and she ducks her head to keep watching—

1 I will use ten dollars to win your entire casino!

Irrashaimase, she says automatically as she approaches him.

I've always wanted to know, what does that actually mean?

He speaks in Mandarin, she is so relieved by this. She's heard the Channel 8 celebrities of his generation speak in English on talk shows, she's felt embarrassed for them.

It means, 'welcome'. Can I take your order, sir?

He looks at her for a moment, perhaps ascertaining if she knows who he is. She wonders why he's alone—his wife is in local showbiz too, a second-tier actress.

Do you have any recommendations?

I've heard the salmon *oyako kamameshi* is good.

You've heard, but not tasted?

No, sir.

Well, your manager should see that his staff knows what their dishes taste like. It'll make you a better waitress.

She says nothing. She wants to say, But I don't want to become a better waitress; I want to believe I will do more with my life.

Very well, I'll try it either way.

She scribbles down the order, gives a small bow and makes her way to the kitchen.

• • •

She serves him the *kamameshi*.

She'd suggested this dish to him because it came with a performative element when served. The server had to place a tiny hourglass—registering a minute of fine white sand—atop the wooden box which concealed the hotplate, where the fish and rice would sizzle. It was just a gimmick, but one that was popular with customers.

You'll have to wait a minute. Be careful when removing the lid—the plate is hot.

Thank you.

She is turning to go, and he has leaned back in his seat. She turns back.

You were always the good guy.

Sorry?

You were always the good guy in the shows. Even when you were the bad guy, you were the good guy.

He laughs. It's true.

Why?

I don't know. They decided I have a good-guy face.

Who?

The directors, producers, demographers.

What are demographers?

They study society and trends to see what people want to watch.

Oh.

The fine sand in the hourglass has trickled down. She indicates this to him with a polite sweep of her hand, and he removes the lid.

O shokuji o o tanoshimi kudasai.

What does that mean?

'Enjoy your meal.'

• • •

He didn't finish the *kamameshi*—perhaps it was a bad recommendation. She really ought to know this, she feels guilty.

She places the wooden box and the cup on her tray, wipes the table with her rag, spreading the smell of damp.

He's gone, but what is she to do. It isn't an autograph that will make her feel better. It isn't as if there's any way for her to tell him what he was to her; is to her. If only she could remove her apron, roll up her shirt, show him the awkward scorch marks from where her mother used the iron on her a decade ago, the period of time coinciding with him playing the blind singer who loses his memory, if only he would say nothing but touch them lightly, trace all seven of them across her ribcage and sternum, then unroll her shirt back down.

She takes the soiled dishes to the back, furtively spooning some rice and beef from his plate, with the spoon he'd used, shoving it into her mouth. The beef is overdone. She licks the spoon, using her teeth and tongue to scrape the congealed grains of rice and gravy on it.

• • •

Fifteen minutes from closing time a phone call to the restaurant's main line, asking for her. The manager hollers for her, trying hard to listen in, pretending to check off the day's reservations at the counter, but he is summoned over by a dissatisfied customer, whose *omu* rice is too soggy.

Hello?

Hello. It's me. The one you recommended the *kamameshi* to.

How did you know my name?

Isn't that what your nametag's for?

Is there something I can help you with?

I'm in a suite in the hotel on top of the casino.

I'm not that sort of girl.

I'm sorry it comes across that way—I just want someone to share the view with. Have you seen things from this high up?

Isn't it funny?

What?

You were in a serial about a casino before there was a casino, and now you're in a hotel suite in a casino.

Life mimics art.

I loved you in that show.

Thank you.

I cried when you had to lick the bad guy's boot. Did you really, or was it a camera trick?

I did it. I was young and I wanted it to feel real.

You won Best Actor for that at the Star Awards that year.

You remember.

I watch everything you're in.

The manager hollers for her to clear a table.

I have to go.

My room number is 2926. You don't have to come up if you don't want to.

• • •

It isn't that she wants to go up, but that she feels compelled to. When you've stared at something out of a box—fibre optics, satellite signals, photons, a piece of furniture—for so long and you're given the chance to feel its edges, the shape of it, it's difficult to not want to touch.

She's changed out of her waitress uniform in the toilet. Her manager asked excitedly, impatiently, all bad breath and yellowed teeth: Who was that? Nobody, she said. She knows right after she leaves, the manager will go around telling all the other wait staff what a slut she is.

She ensures she isn't being followed as she waits for the lift, as she steps in and presses up instead of down.

• • •

Top of the evening news the next day: *King of Caldecott Hill Attempts Suicide in Marina Bay Sands Suite*. Everyone's talking about it, even the Malays and Indians, though he only appears on the Mandarin channel.

Depression, breakdown in marriage, fingers burnt on the stock market, bad investment, lost his life savings at the casino, the rumours are flying. She doesn't care what the reason is, but how could she not have seen this coming?

She sees him as he was in the casino serial: confident and coasting in one scene, in the next tearing off his clothes shouting: "我服输！ 我服输！ 我服输！"[2], humiliated yet a man of honour, keeping his word to the casino kingpin when he's lost the bet, he's forfeited a million dollars in a card game, he's walking out into the night.

• • •

The interrogation room, it's how it looks on the telly, the harsh white light, the one-way window. She's given a glass of water.

2 I admit defeat! I admit defeat! I admit defeat!

What were you doing in Mr Li's room?

We were talking.

What were you talking about?

About the shows he'd been on. I watched them all when I was a kid. About me as a kid.

What is your relationship with Mr Li?

Nothing.

Come again?

We don't have one, in any way.

Why then would he invite you to his hotel room the night before attempting suicide?

I don't know.

You're not being cooperative here. Let's try this again. Why would Mr Li invite you to his hotel room the night before attempting suicide?

I don't know. Because I told him he was always the good guy?

What is this about?

He always played the good guy. On TV.

For how long have you known Mr Li?

I've seen him on TV.

For how long have you known Mr Li personally?

Just last night.

How did you meet?

I'm a waitress at the Japanese restaurant in the hotel. He had dinner there.

How did you end up in his room?

He called the restaurant at closing time.

And?

And asked if I wanted to go up to his room.

Did you and Mr Li engage in sexual activity?

No!

In physical activity, excluding intercourse?

No.

None whatsoever?

Well . . . I showed him my scars.

What scars?

When I was a kid, my mother used to hit me. Sometimes, she used a hot iron.

Where are your scars?

On my ribcage.

Why would you show them to Mr Li?

Because—you wouldn't understand. Please, please let me go. I haven't done anything wrong.

We're just trying to do our job here, ma'am. It looks like a suicide attempt, and we understand from the coroner that the time of death was after you left the room as per the time-stamp on the CCTV, but we need to carry out thorough investigations.

You think I had something to do with his condition?

You were the last person to see him alive. We need to understand what you were doing in his room. The chronology of events. So back to the scars—why would you show them to Mr Li?

When my mother hit me when I was little, I used to imagine that he was my, my father. Or my uncle. Or my older brother. Or my lover. It didn't matter which it was. He was a good guy. He was *the* good guy. He would have protected me. I watched every show he was in. It made me feel closer to him. I felt safe thinking of him. I could imagine him saying my name, putting himself between my mother and me, taking me in his arms, looking at my wounds.

Where was your father?

He left when I was seven. My mother had many men over the years as I was growing up.

Were you, or are you, in love with Mr Li?

(pause) What is love?

(pause) Did you hope to one day be with him?

That's not really love, is it?

(pause) Did you hope to one day meet Mr Li?

No.

Why not?

In my head I already knew him.

(pause) Did Mr Li exhibit any odd behaviour in your company?

No, besides that I thought it odd that he would want to talk to me.

Did he seem emotionally unsound?

No.

What was his behaviour like?

He was calm. Charming. A little wistful.

Did you at any point see the gun, or were you given the knowledge that he had in his possession, the gun?

No.

Do you know that it is illegal to possess a gun in Singapore?

Yes.

Do you know that it is illegal to be in the knowing company of someone in possession of a gun in Singapore?

No.

What time did you leave Mr Li's suite?

I fell asleep and left around nine the following morning.

You shared a bed with Mr Li?

We were lying down and talking, yes.

Were you touching in bed?

No, not at all.

Were you under the covers or over the covers?

How is this question relevant?

Do you know that Mr Li is married?

Yes.

That he has two children?

Yes.

Still you thought it okay to spend the night alone with him in a hotel room.

We were talking.

The CCTV shows that Mr Li gave you money, in the lift.

He gave me twenty bucks to take a cab home.

But you didn't take a cab—you skipped the long line of cabs at the hotel lobby.

Yes, I took a bus home. I'm not rich. I'm not used to taking cabs.

How do we know this monetary exchange wasn't payment for your services?

Because if it was, I wouldn't be so fucking cheap?

Pardon?

Why don't you just check the sheets and his underwear for sperm?

We did.

And?

And there were samples.

Of?

Of male ejaculated bodily fluids.

What? We didn't do a thing.

Why do you think Mr Li invited you to his room?

I think it was because he could feel it.

Feel what?

That I already knew him.

Did he say this?

No.

Then why do you say this?

You asked me what I thought.

• • •

They let her off after three more hours of grilling. They ask if she has anyone to call to pick her up and she says no, she doesn't. On the public bus home, she thinks about his calm smile, his warm hands. The way he propped himself up against a pillow. She thinks about the sperm staining his underwear.

She wants to speak with his wife, to tell her "我们之间没有发生任何关系..."[3] just like on the telly. She wants to bond with his wife over him, to grieve with her.

• • •

Five years later—the way time goes by so conveniently in the last episode of the series, near the end, to make a point, to contextualise a plot turn, to ambiguously tidy up a convoluted

3 There were absolutely no relations or occurrences between us.

and improbable end. Most often it ends with the lead character standing on a breakwater, looking out to the dirty sea—

Just like in the drama serials, he lay in a coma.

Unlike the drama serials, he never got better.

She quit bussing tables at the Japanese restaurant the day after the interrogation. The manager called to let her know there were reporters and photographers lying in wait for her. The manager tried to pry details from her—Well I have to tell the press *something*, don't I?—and she hung up. She didn't bother to chase down her last pay cheque.

She took a second-class degree at a private university and started on a marketing job soon after, marrying a colleague two years later. He was a quiet man who loved her gently. She was happy about this; all she wanted was someone who would never hit her.

Every year on a certain date, she excuses herself to go to the hospice where the King of Caldecott Hill lies, asleep. In all these years, a new King had not been crowned. There were Princes and Queens, but no Kings. There'd been no funeral, no eulogies, no farewell, since he wasn't properly dead.

Sometimes in the afternoons, at odd timings, they still play reruns he starred in. Him at nineteen, at twenty-three, at thirty, at forty-one. The skilled gambler, the patient surgeon, the stoic husband, the anti-hero special agent. Immortalised on film reels, his naturally tanned skin pulled over those cheekbones, the intensity of his gaze. She looks out for these reruns in the telly guide, sets a timer recorder for them. When her husband works late or meets up with his army buddies for a drink, she curls up on the sofa and watches them back to back. "难道我们真的是有缘无份吗？"[4] the King of Caldecott Hill says impetuously to the lead female, index finger curled around her chin, tilting her face to catch the light. She pauses, rewinds, replays.

Half his face was destroyed by the bullet tearing through; it lies in a craggy, floundering mass of skin. His left eye socket droops beyond his non-existent cheekbone, while much of his jaw and lips are a blown-out shipwreck.

It hadn't shocked her at all, from the outset. She'd asked the nurse if she could touch. The nurse had asked her relationship to him; she said it was complicated. She touched.

Over the past year, his hair began turning white. She finds this alarming, and brings with her on her next visit a box of hair dye from the pharmacy. The nurse accedes, proffering her old towels to line his shoulders, and a C-shaped shoulder-resting basin to catch drips.

As they wait for the hair dye to be absorbed by his roots—and it is wondrous to imagine that in there, a part of him is still capable of absorption, as it were—the nurse says to her in an undertone: This means that *she* will know there's someone else who visits him.

Who?

His wife.

She hasn't thought of this, to be honest. Of course she's always feared bumping into the wife at the hospice, but she always manages to convince herself to chance it. On every

4 How is it possible that we were fated only to meet, but not destined to be together?

visit, she makes sure to position herself with a view of the long corridor, and she's long familiarised herself with the swiftest exit route from the other side of the room.

How often does she come?

Once every two or three months. She comes with the children.

What do they do?

Talk to him a little, talk amongst themselves. Show him old photographs. They stay around twenty minutes each time.

Tell her you did it, won't you? That you coloured his hair? It was a leftover from another patient's and you didn't want it to go to waste.

The nurse is silent, but it feels like acquiescence. They both watch the King of Caldecott Hill, breathing measuredly via the respirator. Sometimes when she watches him for too long, she thinks she sees a finger of his twitching.

• • •

In every Chinese drama serial, there comes a point where the male lead raises his eyes to the heavens, holds up three fingers and attempts to swear his eternal love for the female lead. Lest he proves untrue, he invokes, with a Chinese idiom, celestial retribution and certain death—"如果我, xxx, 做出任何对不起 xxx 的事，我将会被天打雷劈。"[5] The female lead, being Chinese and superstitious, fears the attraction of misfortune and never allows the male lead to complete the utterance of this line, often pulling down the raised hand coyly,

5 If I, xxx, do unto xxx any manner of betrayal, may the heavens punish me via lightning striking me down dead.

in feminine concern mixed in with shy delight at his willingness to demonstrate devotion.

Doesn't he look better now, she says as she gently towels his hair dry, the smell of ammonia permeating the ward. Still so handsome, isn't he? The nurse bites her lip. Don't worry, she says to the nurse, I'm not kidding myself that he'll ever come to.

She touches her scars through her blouse, all seven of them, one by one, each with a different finger. That was how he'd done it when she was twenty-one, when she'd lifted up her shirt, as if he'd sat down to a piano to practise a scale. She swallows and remembers the stock line she'd seen and heard the King of Caldecott Hill utter so many times, through the years, as his onscreen lover would draw her last breath, courtesy of a car accident; a brain tumour; a knifing by a psychopath; that misty glaze to his eyes, the same way his voice would catch in the back of his throat each time: "不管天长地久，只需曾经拥有。"[6]

6 Eternity is not the crux; the only necessary knowledge is that we once possessed each other.

Every Park on This Island

Bukit Timah Hill

The Bear says: We had a forest in our backyard. It caught fire one summer.

The Bear says: I never finished exploring it.

The Bear says: Well, what I mean is it was eleven acres.

He'd asked, casually, if we had nature trails here in Singapore. I said we could try Bukit Timah Hill, and then I realised I'd asked him out, but right before I froze up he said, Sure. Looking for directions there, I come across a factoid: that it is the highest point on this island, at an altitude of 163.63 metres. It makes me feel funny, because when I imagine the word altitude, I imagine thin air, the need to acclimatise.

He opens up his bag—knapsack, he says—and takes out a Ziploc.

For you. Trail mix.

It's a mixture of almonds, raisins, peanuts, M&Ms and granola, and somehow I think it's the sweetest thing ever.

We sit on the root of a tree sharing the trail mix, watching fat red ants go by. He tells me that on his boyhood nature trails in Pennsylvania, they would see white-tailed deer and red foxes. A small chameleon appears and crosses in front of us slowly, like some sort of visual cue or subtitle. I find myself laughing.

Somehow he gets it, and laughs too, a deep, throaty laugh.

I've never made a special trip to any park or hill in Singapore, I say as we part at the bus stop. I sure can tell, he says. Which girl would wear stuff like that to hike? The Bear points to my vintage T-straps, my sweetheart-neckline sundress.

Hike? When the hill is less than two hundred metres tall and the routes are all paved? I say. I must take you to Fort Canning Park one day—there's an escalator built *into* the side of the hill, can you imagine that?

How about, he says, We go to every park on this island.

Every park on this island?

Every park on this island.

Clementi Woods

When I get home to my tenth floor flat in Clementi Woods, I boot my laptop up. On this island that calls itself a garden city, there are twelve city and heritage parks, thirteen community parks, six coastal parks, five southern ridge parks, six nature parks, four nature reserves, seven riverine parks, the Botanic Gardens, the Zoological Gardens, and the Gardens by the Bay. I draw up a map, mark them all out, and pin it to the corkboard above my desk.

Over dinner, I ask my parents for the land area of our flat. *Land* area, of our tenth floor flat, the same strange rhythm as "an *altitude* of 163.63 metres". It makes me feel, all of a sudden, that all these years I have been walking on air, that each block of flats is a soufflé of sorts. All the air that passes through windows, balconies, open doors: we're layered atop one another, whipped into a social dough. The Cantopop karaoke beat from not one, but three floors down, the smell of rendang curry from the adjacent kitchen window of a Malay family.

About seven hundred square feet, my mother says. Why?

I don't answer her. I do an online conversion. 700 square feet = 0.0160697888 acres.

Singapore Zoological Gardens

My parents like to tell this story, of me crying over bears when I was a kid.

Bears had been my favourite animal. I had books with big brown bears, who had little potbellies and ate honey out of jars, who stood upright. I had a stuffed teddy bear I slept next to at night.

When we went to the zoo for the first time, I was beside myself with excitement. I ignored everything else we passed—flamingos, golden tamarins, zebras, lions. We got to the sun bear enclosure and my father lifted me up under the arms for a better look.

It was not large, nor brown, nor furry. It reminded me of the dark spots on the skin of an overripe banana, and I began to cry.

When I first saw the Bear, I went right up behind him. He was standing by the vending machine outside a lecture theatre on campus, frowning. He was very tall; big-boned and pudgy, with a paunch showing slightly under his black t-shirt, and soft, wavy honey brown hair just past his shoulders.

I couldn't figure out what it was about him—there were better looking white boys on the exchange programme and local boys around that I'd never stopped to stare at—but there I was right behind him, and then I realised I'd found my picture-book bear.

He turned around. Tough luck, he muttered, shrugging. The vending machine had eaten his coins without dispensing his item. He was walking away.

I kicked the vending machine—perhaps that was the first time I'd kicked anything my whole life. The packet of M&Ms fell into the dispenser gutter. He turned back and I was ready to hand it over to him. I could feel my face shining.

Thanks, he said. He didn't look impressed. For a moment he looked as if he was going to walk away again, then he told me his name. I won't say it, because to me he will forever simply be the Bear.

I told him my name back, a Chinese name, and he said right away, I'm going to have to give you a new name, girl.

I stared dumbly back at him.

The Bear said: Besides the fact that I'll never be able to pronounce it, it's soft and . . . gospel. You need something more hard-hitting if you don't want to blend in with the wallpaper.

He turned to me, checking—You don't, right? I knew I had always been a wallpaper type of girl, I was quiet and if I stood out it was only because the other girls thought I was weird in my vintage dresses and shoes and my significant (if useless) knowledge of Pre-Code Hollywood—I might be wrong but maybe only *certain* types of girls can pull off vintage, one of them had said to her posse as I walked past them once.

The Bear was snapping his fingers.

Sledgehammer, he said.

I loved it. It was time for me to say something, and I thought it through, and pushed my spectacles up my nose bridge and inhaled before I said it: You talk like the movies.

The Bear grinned wildly at me, with large white teeth. He opened the packet of M&Ms and gave me a red one, himself a blue.

Telok Blangah Hill Park

Is everything they say about New York City true?

What's everything?

I don't know, but everyone wants to go to New York, don't they?

I'll have you know I hail west of the Appalachians and I don't know anything east of it.

So you've never been to New York?

Just once, and to be honest it's not unlike Singapore, in a way.

What? That can't be true.

Well, what I mean is—where I'm from, there aren't any skyscrapers or subway systems. Cities are cities. They're exciting in their own ways. You just don't know it 'cause you grew up in one.

Tell me something exciting about Singapore, then.

It's very walkable—from the museums to the malls—and all those city lights—and you see all kinds of people—

Except we don't have anything real in those museums and the malls are all alike.

—and the Indian temples and the hawker centres and the old men drinking beer in the afternoons and laksa and fried cockles for two dollars?

I can't give up now, so I keep talking: How about thrift stores? Do you have thrift stores, chockfull of pleated circle skirts and tea dresses? And diners? And five-and-dimes? And peepshows?

The Bear stops walking. He turns to me and puts his hands on my damp shoulders, and then he laughs, kindly.

Sledge, d'you know something? There isn't an airport in my town. To get to the nearest mall, you pretty much need to have a car, and it'll be a half hour drive there. It's only four storeys high, and the entire first level is a Walmart. Can you even imagine that? Nothing ever happens in your town, so you assume nothing happens in the whole wide world. I wish I could stay here forever.

Lower Peirce Reservoir

Tell me something about Pennsylvania.

We're the snack food capital of the world. That's how I got fat.

Really?

Yeah. Hershey's and Auntie Anne's and Mars bars and all the major potato chip manufacturers all have their headquarters in Pennsylvania.

What else?

We've the second highest number of black bears in all of America.

Bears?

Yeah, bears. We hunt them.

You've used a gun?

A hunting rifle, yeah.

Did you kill anything?

Mostly turkey and grouse. We saw a bear once, my dad and I, and we took pot shots at it, but it was too fast for us.

Don't you feel bad?

Aw shucks, Sledge, don't look at me that way.

Mount Faber

Well I've always found this embarrassing.

What, Sledge?

The fact that this hill of 105 metres is called Mount Faber. Isn't that really embarrassing? What would the Andes and the Alps think?

It's just a name.

No, it isn't, it's punching above one's weight.

Small people need to talk more loudly to be heard.

Well I'm small aren't I, I'm not even 1.6 metres tall, but you don't see me raising my voice.

Maybe you're okay with not being heard.

I just want to be heard by the right people. The right person.

Ang Mo Kio Park

We're walking through the park quietly and there are two people at the edge of a bougainvillea bush, making out, and when the man moans, I say, If a tree falls in a forest and no one is there to hear it, does it make a sound?

What d'you mean?

I mean, I want their moment to belong to them.

The Bear teases, You mean you aren't a voyeur?

It's not that, I say as we walk away. Do you know that from my room, I can hear someone sneeze from the block opposite mine? And when the kid upstairs gets caned by his father, I can hear him cry?

Can I tell you about my gran? She was a flapper—y'know what that is?

Of course. I would kill to be in the Roaring Twenties.

Right. So my gran, born and bred in New York before she met my gramp, who was a trucker passing through. She fell in love and they moved to the Midwest. In the end, as my dad tells it, she never forgave my gramps for it.

What do you mean?

She never forgave him for taking her away from the city. She hated how quiet it got. No music, no dancehalls, no fashion, no cafés, no scuffles, no banter.

What happened then?

What could she do? She had my dad and my uncles and became a suburban housewife. When I was a kid, she was ancient, but I remember her putting on these old jazz records on the gramophone.

My grandmother was a samsui woman.

What's that?

That means she wore a red headdress on her head and carried heavy loads off of ships that were meant for men.

So they were both pioneers of their time, kinda. Your gran carrying heavy loads by the dock and my gran burning up the dance floor.

Did she keep her flapper dresses? Did she have the hair of

Louise Brooks?

Everyone had the hair of Louise Brooks. When she died, I was ten. They had a small estate sale and they sold off her stuff: the dresses she'd kept, her shoes, her hats, her records. I remember this one woman with green eyes buying up all of her dresses.

I could slap you.

You're so weird, Sledge.

I'm sorry.

No sweetie, I meant it as a compliment.

Bishan Park

Sledge, teach me all the bad words in Hokkien.

But I don't even use any of them.

That's not true, I've heard you say *wa lau eh*.

Hey, that's just like—oh my god.

So teach me the really nasty stuff.

Okay. *Chao chee bye*.

Chao chee bye. What's that?

Stinking vagina.

Good one.

Don't use it in front of me.

I won't. Next?

Ka ni na.

Ka ni na.

That's fuck your mother. And then there's *lan pa*.

Lan pa. Dickhead?

Close—balls. Dick is *lan jiao*.

Lan jiao.

More forceful on the *jiao*.

Lan jiao!

That's it.

Botanic Gardens

It's in a gazebo in the Botanic Gardens that he puts his hand on my knee, and by the time the sun sets, it's on my thigh. He just leaves it there, inanimate, and we go on talking.

Is it true that you guys have drive-through weddings in Las Vegas?

Sure—not that I've participated in any, though.

What do you think of them?

I don't believe in marriage.

Well neither do I, unless it's with a 99-cent thrift store ring.

Ha-ha.

No, I'm serious!

Well then you're my kind of girl.

You're being cheap.

Naw, I'm being anti-consumerist.

It's just I don't think marriage should be about the flash and splash.

You're a gem, Sledge. A 99-cent thrift store ring, and some apple pie to go with it.

Changi Beach Park

We outdo ourselves on our twenty-fourth park visit: we've brought a little picnic mat and our own sandwiches, ham and cheese on white bread slapped with margarine. When the Bear chooses a soft patch of grass half obscured by a bush rather than the sand closer to the coastline, I know what it means, I only don't know when to begin. He makes it easy for me by putting an arm around me before we even unwrap our sandwiches, and soon I've unzipped his fly.

It's dark, and it's the first penis I've seen, the first penis I've touched, and I tell myself to do my best as I remove my spectacles and bend my head over.

He's touching me all over and I lay back as he pulls my panties down to my knees, but then he stops, and already his penis is becoming flaccid, even with my fingers still steadfastly around it, and I feel like a small animal just died in my hands because I handled it the wrong way.

What's wrong?

He's looking at me, then looking away.

You're a great girl, he says. I—I don't want an easy lay.

I shock myself by saying: What makes you think I don't want it as much as you do?

He puts his head back between his hands. His hair falls forward across his bulky shoulders, a curtain of golden brown.

I don't know how to say this, but I think I can only do it with white girls.

Clementi Woods

There are only twenty-six weeks in six months, and there'd always been fifty-six parks on this island. He'd a month left of his exchange programme and we had thirty-one parks to go.

He calls me and I let it ring and die off each time. Sometimes

I pick up and let him say *Hello*. I don't let him get to *Hello, Sledge?* As it's always been, the boys don't look at me. The girls call me by my Chinese name, treat me like a weirdo or a wallflower, someone to ignore or to trail in their wake. I'd always been happy on my own, but now I surround myself with them, any of them who'll have me in their little cliques so I'm never alone in school, so he never comes up to me. When the girls say *Who's that fat ang moh dude staring at us? What a creep*, I laugh right along. They talk about American indie bands, school, the boys they are seeing, the best brand for nail polish that doesn't chip. They tell me I should get contact lenses and a tan, that vintage was trendy last season but it's so over now. *Where on earth do you get your clothes from anyway?* eBay, I say, I stay up late to activate my reserve bid sometimes, and they roar with laughter and send me links to Urban Outfitters and the best local blogshops.

Every night, I replay the things he's told me, matching it always to the parks we were in.

Pearl's Hill City Park: My brothers tied me to an old yule tree, and there was a hornet's nest nearby. If I didn't untie myself in time, I would have died.

Toa Payoh Town Park: We went into the forest on reconnaissance missions. We would take turns to steal each others' most valuable treasure, hide it in the thick of the woods, and create a treasure map. I got bitten by a snake whilst retrieving my nutcracker, and my brother broke a leg getting his T. rex back from a high treetop.

Little Guilin: We'd seen a flying fox in the forest. I was thinking of the flying fox when I leapt from the top of the bunk bed. I was meant to reach the embankment of the other bunk bed. Next thing I knew, I'd hit the floor and the corner of the antique dresser was in my mouth. My mother came in, arms akimbo, and demanded, What's going on? My brothers remained silent. I opened my mouth to say, Nothing, but blood volleyed out and five of my milk teeth plopped onto the floor like stray marbles.

Clementi Woods

He's waiting under my block, by the tiled table that the old men play chess at.

Sledge, he says, please.

I walk past him towards the lift and he enters it with me.

Sledge, I leave in three days.

So?

I don't want things to be like that between us. Can't we still be friends?

Does it matter? We'll never see each other again.

The slightly sweet, slightly sour smell of his sweat is in the air, and I feel myself wavering, as he says, Will you go to one last park with me?

East Coast Park

The sea breeze is sticky on our faces and salty on our tongues. Forgiveness isn't as difficult as we make believe, it's the impossibility of forgetting that inspires fear. The Bear sits to my left and we're talking like we've always talked; we order char kway teow, sambal stingray, oyster omelette, satay, calamansi juice and Tiger beer. It's past midnight but the hawker centre by the beach is crowded and we're both getting a bit tipsy.

Can I ask you something?

Sure.

Are you sure you're sure?

Yeah.

Were you a loser in America?

He turns to me and I look for hurt in his face.

I mean—I don't think you're a loser!—but as a kid, here, I read stuff like *Sweet Valley High*, I watched *Dawson's Creek*. You're not a jock, and I'm not a cheerleader. So that makes us losers, right?

Right.

We're both quiet, looking out at the empty cyclist paths, and the Bear says, I used to get laughed at for always having my nose in a book; for being fat. I don't know how bad the bullying here gets, but trust me, if you were a loser and you survived public school in America, you'll survive anything else. It's comforting, in a way.

I'm sorry I asked.

No, don't be.

For what it's worth, I still think you're a great guy.

He looks over at me and smiles. Sledge, you're such a softie.

He orders us one more round of beer—One for the road! The Bear announces cheerily—and seconds of oyster omelette and char kway teow.

I'm not going to get any more of this back in Pennsylvania, the Bear says as he picks at the lard and the bean sprouts in the greasy noodles. What do you call the oyster omelette again?

Or luak. What do you eat back home?

We're famous for our cheesesteaks and hoagie, but they should get a load of or luak.

I'm on my third beer and the Bear is on his fifth. The Bear, quite drunk now, says: I can't believe I didn't get laid in Singapore.

The Bear says: Could you hook me up with *that* sort of girl?

He's pointing indiscreetly at a fair-skinned Chinese girl two plastic tables away: long, rebonded hair highlighted gold, false eyelashes and thick eyeliner over single eyelids, ample cleavage spilling out of a halter top, denim shorts so short I can see the rise of her butt cheeks, legs ending in kitten heels.

That's an ah lian.

Ah lian? He says it funny, and claps me on the back. You guys are so funny. I didn't know there was a name for girls like that. That's neat.

The ah lian turns and on the smooth skin of her exposed back is a large Kwan Yin tattoo. As she raises her mug of beer, her shoulder blade moves, rippling the inked skin. The Bear points again.

What's her tattoo of?

It's the Buddhist Goddess of Mercy.

Does that mean she's religious?

No, it means she's in a gang.

Well, I wouldn't say no to that.

She's walking over now, with three identical boys in muscle tees and baggy jeans and flip flops, tattooed arms and hair dyed the colour of harvest wheat—ah bengs. The Bear doesn't know that you don't point at girls like that.

She speaks in Mandarin.

Why are you two talking about me?

What makes you think we're talking about you.

Don't give me any bullshit—I saw him pointing at me.

He said he wants to fuck you.

Kaninachaocheebyenabei—

The ah lian slaps me, and the ah bengs are unloosed on the Bear like a pack of dogs.

I don't hit back. I adjust my spectacles, and after casting me a hard look under her mascara and false lashes, she stands beside me without animosity. We watch the fight casually, the Bear on the ground and the ah bengs kicking his face in. They stop when the sambal stingray hawker shouts, *Wa pat den wa hor* police *liao, mai luan luan lai!* She removes her kitten heels, slings them in hand, and they run towards the car park.

His eye is like a grape that's been stepped on, and he's groaning.

Sledge.

Yes?

It hurts.

I know.

I help him up, he's heavy—as a bear should be—and we get into a cab. We don't wait for the police.

In the cab, he leans his head on my shoulder. On the radio is a silly, upbeat Chinese song, popular with teenaged girls here several years ago. The lyrics go, *I love you, loving you, like the mouse loves the rice grain.* It doesn't sound half as stupid in Mandarin, in the saccharine voice of the Taiwanese pop star.

Inexplicably, the Bear begins feeling me up. I don't stop him.

When the cab reaches his hostel, he reaches out for his

wallet to pay but I say, Uncle, one more location, to indicate that I am not getting out with him. The Bear staggers out of the cab with his beaten face. I shut the door, and the cab driver pulls away.

Clementi Woods

Once, a frog that lived in a well bragged to a turtle that lived in the sea.

"I am so happy!" cried the frog, "When I go out, I jump about on the railing around the edge of the well. When I come home, I rest in the holes inside the wall of the well. If I jump into the water, it comes all the way up to my armpits and I can float on my belly. If I walk in the mud, it covers up my flippered feet. I look around at the wriggly worms, crabs and tadpoles, and none of them can compare with me. I am lord of this well and I stand tall here. My happiness is great. My dear sir, why don't you come more often and look around my place?"

Before the turtle from the sea could get its left foot in the well, its right knee got stuck. It hesitated and retreated. The turtle told the frog about the sea.

"Even a distance of a thousand miles cannot give you an idea of the sea's width; even a height of a thousand metres cannot give you an idea of its depth. In the time of the great floods, the waters in the sea did not increase. During the terrible droughts, the waters in the sea did not decrease. The sea does not change along with the passage of time and its level does not rise or fall according to the amount of rain that falls. The greatest happiness is to live in the sea."

After listening to these words, the frog of the shallow well was shocked into the realisation of his own insignificance and became very ill at ease.

In my dreams, the Bear says: Come with me, I'll pull you out of burning houses. I'll fashion you a canoe from wood, in my father's tool shed. This is the Chinese parable I tell the Bear in return, to explain to him that I can never leave, not because I think the most of my environs, but that my environs have become me.

In my dreams, the Bear says, sadly: So you'll never leave that island of yours?

In my dreams, I reply: You were the closest thing to leaving.

Six months after the Bear leaves I get a parcel in the mail, wrapped in brown paper, tied in white twine.

It's a flapper dress, and except for a small discolouration at the hem and the loss of a few beads at the neckline detail, it is Roaring Twenties perfection. How could I, an ordinary Asian girl on a humid island, ever wear it?

As I crush the brown paper out slides a photograph. Louise Brooks hair, a cloche hat, a slouchy silhouette, shin-high socks. She has his eyes. Or rather, the Bear has her eyes. On the back he's written: *I'm sorry we didn't get to go to every park on your island.*

The dress is jammed to the back of my cupboard, but I can't stop thinking about it.

I take the picture of the Bear's grandmother to the neighbourhood saloon and tell the hairdresser auntie this is what I want. Wah, where you get this photo? she wants to know as she takes it from me with long nails the colour of aubergines. From a photo album in Salvation Army, I say.

Eh, *pantang*! She says the Malay word for bad luck and drops the photograph back in my lap. As she reaches over for a nylon gown to lay around me, I see her clasping her hands together towards the small red Buddhist altar she has in the corner, the golden bodhisattva idol on a lotus flower.

She botches the haircut, right before my eyes, and I let it happen. She shows me the back view of her handiwork with a large round mirror, and tells me how this bob with dipped ends is *very fashion now ah girl, auntie give you the best.* My hands gripping the photograph of the Bear's flapper grandmother are turning white. I pay and leave.

When I get home, I put on the flapper dress slowly, careful not to snag it. It fits like a dream. I take a Polaroid—the old Polaroid, not the Fuji Instax variety—of myself in the mirror. The flash obscures three-quarters of my face, the camera the last quarter.

I remove the dress, pull on shorts and a t-shirt, take the lift down. I have the flapper dress and the photograph of the Bear's grandmother with me. The large metal prayer bin isn't in use, it isn't a Buddhist or Taoist-observed day of the month. I drop the dress and the photograph into the prayer bin. I buy a matchbook from the provision store under the block, light all the matches, one by one, let them fall in. I don't wait to see it burn up. Home, I pick up the Polaroid and write on the border:

Where am I going to get another boy here who understands that I want to get married with a 99-cent thrift store ring?

As I drop the addressed and stamped Polaroid off in the mailbox the next day, I think to myself that if I were the Pennsylvanian mailman and one hot afternoon I stopped to breathe, to see this, I might fall a little in love with me, for all of one minute—checking the postage stamp: all the way from

Singapore, where's that, on the Southern tip of China?—before I went on my way, past the deserted town roads and the blue, blue skies.

Two Ways To Do This

ZUROTUL WAS MADE for love, only she was born in the wrong environs for love to occur.

She had come through the cargo hold of a ship rather than a plane because this was cheaper—she wouldn't have to pay off the placement fee for as long as if she'd taken a plane. She'd sat in a corner and, at some point, threw up in her own lap; there were still bits of tempeh on her skirt though she'd tried her best to clean it off onto the exterior of a gunny sack stuffed with tubers.

She wasn't one of those who sought city life, who wanted something better, larger. She was happiest in the padi fields and she worked harder than the old family ox. But she'd been bathing in the river when the four men came, and when they were done with her, she lay naked and sacked on the mud of the riverbank, shaking uncontrollably. They were laughing as they left, and the last man turned back briefly to give her a kick in the ribs as a parting shot.

Step up.

A Chinese woman who could speak Bahasa Indonesia was asking for her name, taking her weight and height. She'd lost much weight after the rape. The woman peered at the scales and muttered that she'd bump up the figure on paper—*too heavy or too light and they'll think you eat lots of rice. Then they won't want to hire you.* They were given lawn-green polo shirts to change into. The shirts read *Happy Maid Employment Services Pte Ltd* on the back. There was a collapsible banner right outside the agency's storefront with the picture of a local celebrity on it; the one who cross-dressed for comedic skits on talk shows, made inane movies and, most recently, cheated on his wife. He was grinning. He had one arm around a smiling maid in an apron, the other held in front of his chest in a thumbs up.

Zurotul would never go home—it was no longer home. When she told her father what had happened, his face had remained impassive. Then he told her to marry her rapist. But there were four of them, she said. He stroked his beard as she sat at his feet, waspishly contemplating the complication of chronology: how should the prospective husband then be ascertained? Her mother was crying silently. That night, she packed up a scant little bundle and left before dawn broke, holding in the urge to kiss the hands of her sleeping mother and her five siblings.

Some days she would wake in the holding dorm and smell rancid breath shot through with cheap toddy hanging over her. She'd hasten to the bathroom, splashing cool water on her face, brushing her teeth till her gums bled, anything to stave off the nausea. She'd look at her face in the mirror, touch her own reflection.

There are some women, whom, having been raped, or whilst being raped, wish to die. Zurotul wasn't one of them. Even as they were taking turns with her, from the back to the front to the back again, the fluid shape in the middle of her mind shifted from a piteous anguish to a *gladness* that, thus far, they weren't threatening to take her life, and that in all likelihood she would survive this. The sky was very beautiful that dawn, and she found she was able to take comfort in this. She stopped clawing at the men even as they pawed at her crudely. Her pupils were dilated and she found she had an almost preternatural sense of sight and sound. Somewhere a bird was making a low, insistent hooting call for a mating partner. Her body was moving beneath her and she was no longer resisting. Her arms were open like the Madonna, her gaze skyward.

Smile, no teeth.

They were having their pictures taken for potential employees to look at. They were told to smile faintly—nothing too gregarious. There was a girl who didn't want to have her picture taken, who was afraid of the camera, as if it were a gun. Soul-snatching, she muttered over and over in Jawa Serang, each time the flash went off.

Zurotul took the hand of this girl, and stroked her head. This girl had lice in her hair when she came, and the maid agency had sheared her head, terrified of a dorm-wide infection. The crew cut felt good under Zurotul's hand. The girl was coaxed into having her picture taken, even offering up a watery smile directed at Zurotul, who stood beside the porky Chinese man with the camera.

Following this, Wati adhered herself to Zurotul like a barnacle, blabbering to her about her village and her family and her apprehensions all day. Wati was young; she had not yet known men. She climbed into Zurotul's bunk at night and held her tight, with an earnest innocence.

One night, six days in, Zurotul said gently in Jawa Serang: Wati, you know this is temporary, right?

What is?

This place, this bed. Me.

Wati, who knew nothing, thought Zurotul was being cruel, and chided her before bursting into tears and crawling back to her bunk bed.

Zurotul's first instinct was to follow Wati into her bed, to comfort the girl whose crew cut had grown out into small tight ringlets, which were quite comely. Then she considered the life that lay before her, and it seemed almost impudent to think about forming attachments to anything; why would she start now? She was now a maid. She would perform chores—clean up after someone, tidy a house—but love was not on the cards. The agents had said as much: no boyfriend, or you get sent home. No handphone unless your ma'am and sir say okay.

In the village, she'd had a cluster of friends who twittered like hens about nothing in particular and she'd played games with her siblings involving cotton pods and saga seeds and twigs and hemp rope. She was always the one listening, always the one twirling the rope, never the one jumping. Sometimes when she thought about it, it felt *reasonable* to her that she was raped—someone needed something, and she was in a position to give it. She wondered, if it'd been only one man raping her and if her father had similarly suggested her hand in marriage, would she have complied with his wishes? She thinks she would have, and then always, she tries to quell the brimming thought there, because if it spills, the question is this—would she have learned to love her rapist?

This is how you cradle a baby.

Absurdly, they'd been given naked baby dolls, moulded of cheap plastic, peach-coloured, with false eyelashes that fluttered shut over coloured irises when you cradled them at an angle.

Zurotul held the featherweight approximation of a child patiently, remembering fondly her younger sister as a baby, how she would fan a dried banana leaf to keep her cool, how her sister tried to locate a nipple on her when she held her near her chest. Wati was standing loftily away from her, holding the doll in an awkward position. The Chinese woman was walking around with a clipboard, adjusting the crooks of their elbows and wrists to best support the doll.

Soon they were versed cursorily in domestic chores—the ironing of clothes, the boiling of water, the operation of a vacuum cleaner, the scrounging of a sink, the folding of long-sleeved shirts—as well as basic English phrases: good morning, sir, good morning, ma'am, sorry, yes, I don't eat pork, I don't understand, could you explain again, I understand, sorry, sorry. They were rounded up to sit in a neat row on the faux leather-padded benches at the reception area of the agency, where prospective employers might find favour with their appearances.

The woman walked in right before the man—in fact she was holding his hand—but it was only the man Zurotul saw. If she'd seen the woman, she would have noticed the supercilious curl of her lip, the perfect perm, chestnut-coloured, with no dark roots showing.

But it was the man she saw, that spoke to the capacity for love she'd always, always held inside her. His face was unremarkable, a little horsey, but in the sea of lawn-green polo shirts, his eyes had immediately clapped onto hers, and for no reason in particular, he smiled a winning smile at her. His teeth were large and yellow, but it was the decisive generosity of the smile that took her in, that pulled her under, in waters she'd thought would remain placid forever, the impassive calm of the lake as she was raped. It was the sort of smile someone might lavish upon his returning lover or child at the arrival hall of an airport terminal, after a long absence. She held her breath as he surveyed the rest of the room, as his wife sat down on the stool before the counter—the sweeping gaze he'd cast the rest of the maids with was cursory; he'd not extended that same smile to them.

They went through paper profiles together. From the way the wife's jaw moved and the expression on the agent's face, Zurotul could see she was asking hard questions. The man had a patient expression on his face. After a third of an hour, the agent called out the names: Wati. Zurotul.

Wati's hair had grown out, bunching around her head like a Southeast Asian Botticelli cherub. Zurotul found herself adjusting the rubber band that held her hair. The wife stepped around them gingerly, asking the agent questions in English. The husband lingered—it seemed—with a sort of decorum that implied that they—the prospective maids—were human, rather than fruit or livestock up for inspection, and for this Zurotul was grateful. She found herself thinking too quickly that she would do anything for this man. She imagined the great and simple pleasure it would be to lift his well-worn bedroom slippers by the bed to sweep under them; to lay out matching socks on leather work shoes she'd have polished to a shine the night before.

The wife turned to the husband to say, Well?

The husband indicated with a hand—rather than a finger—his choice: Zurotul. Wati had taken to placing her hands slightly akimbo, as if this might be a pageant of sorts. Zurotul left her arms limp by her sides as she smiled nervously at the husband.

The wife said: Well, I prefer the other. She pointed to Wati with a manicured index finger. The husband opened his mouth to ask why, and Zurotul saw the large teeth. The wife folded her arms and cocked her head.

She looks fresher. That one looks used.

Ma'am, this batch of domestic helpers are all new, the agent said quickly. They come straight from West Java and we train them on-site.

The wife rolled her eyes.

I don't mean it literally. I just don't like her face.

Zurotul could not understand what was being said, and her nails were biting into the sides of her thighs. She looked at Wati, whose hands were still on her hips.

The wife and the agent turned towards the husband, expectant. Whatever you say, dear, he said. The wife, satisfied, turned her back on the prospective maids, and settled back down on the stool. The man looked at Zurotul for a moment. She'd seen the look before, but she wasn't sure where.

The husband and wife signed papers. Neither Zurotul nor Wati could sense conclusively what the decision was, until the agent told Wati to go pack her belongings. Later, over dinner, Wati sauntered into the crowded back kitchen like a homecoming queen. The other unchosen maids were congratulating her, hugging her in turn and whispering well-wishes into her ear.

Zurotul was made for love, but she was also born to lose. What surprised her wasn't that she wasn't picked; what surprised her was that she still had it in her to want things. She'd felt earthly desire ebb—from her heart through to her limbs, into the soil, and she knew, finally, at some point, to leech into the lake—as she had been raped. As the dawn segued into a clear, humid morning and she lay motionless for hours, she knew then what it was like to be a vessel. Life would be easy from then on, because she'd been given to know what emptiness was. This is what Theravada Buddhist monks give up verbal speech for. This is why Hindu ascetics put up one arm for ten years and allow it to atrophy. The piety of transcendence conferred upon Zurotul through utter violation—not the violation in and of itself but the verity that after the most painful and demeaning thing in the world had happened to her, *she was still there*—not devotional apotheosis; by a crime of opportunity—that the four men had probably already forgotten about, that no one in her village was going to be punished for—not self-cultivation.

Make no mistake—for what she'd wanted wasn't the man, wasn't his smile. What she'd wanted was to be *of use* to him. It was unclear if Zurotul herself could draw such distinctions, if she *would* draw such distinctions. For Zurotul, love was still that all-consuming passion and deference. It was straightforwardness, but it wasn't stupidity. It was easy, but it wasn't loose. Not every girl from the village was like this, but Zurotul was special. Just one well-played smile and she could be yours forever; the tragedy was that you might never even know it.

After Wati left, a few of the maids, Zurotul included, were selected to be given special training in assisting in the daily care of the elderly or bedridden. The owner of the agency had read in the papers, not too long ago, of the impending silver tsunami—he'd thought this a melodramatic way of referring to the ageing population—and was trying to carve out an early-adopter niche for Happy Maid Employment Services Pte Ltd.

This is how you clean the soiled behind of the bedridden.

It was a gender-neutral life-sized dummy, the type Red Cross Corps practise CPR on, and they had smeared its durable elastomer bottom with something brown and pulpy, but it didn't smell. Zurotul remembered the sharp stink of the village hag with the sleepy sickness in the west end of the village, who had lived in the shrine secreted behind heavy vegetation. You could smell her from a mile away, and because no one ever went near, the village hag, in her solitude, took on mystic properties. Her mystique was of the variety that went untapped—she did not predict droughts or favourable crops, nor dole out poisons or folk remedies.

Right before she left her village for the city, Zurotul was compelled to pay the village hag a visit. She stumbled through thick vegetation and saw a king cobra two feet ahead of her, just as the decrepit hut came into view. It rose and spread its hood. Zurotul dropped to her knees and lowered her head, as her mother had told them to, as children. When she raised her eyes, the cobra was gone.

She entered the hut and the smell was unimaginable, even for someone like Zurotul, who bathed in a river where, further upstream, another village defecated into the same river.

She persisted without holding a hand to her nose—it seemed so ill-mannered. The village hag was lying on a rotting plank of wood on the floor of the hut, partially in her own faecal matter. It was obvious she was dying. There were septic wounds on her legs that black flies had already begun descending upon.

You came, the village hag said, eyes closed.

Zurotul was trying not to cry. She wished the village had devised a system of care for the hag, or that someone had stepped forward to call on her. She tucked her legs under her and reached out to hold the hag's hand, already cold.

I'm sorry, she said.

Don't be, the hag said, smiling toothlessly, *I'm glad you came.*

How did you know I was coming?

I've known it since the day you were born, the hag said, squeezing her hand weakly. *Nether blood on a full moon will win his heart.*

She would never remember it, but this was where she'd seen the look on the husband's face: it was the look on the village hag's face as she was dying. It wasn't that Zurotul had forgotten the village hag's dying face, only that the two—the Chinese husband and the village hag—seemed so far removed that she would never think to draw the correlation. Their faces both read: *this is out of my hands; life is out of my hands.*

What no one had told Zurotul was that when she was born, the village hag had passed the crude bounds of her familial longhouse, hatched with branches, and demanded a drink of water. Because she was toothless—her mouth a small, mirthless black hole—and her breath exceedingly fecund, Zurotul's older sister, then seven, who was not learned in the unspoken hierarchies of the village, had squealed in horror and refused her.

The hag had looked delighted as the guileless girl skipped away, as if it were a welcoming overture. She spat on the ground—her spit an alarming shade of sorrel—grinned at the retreating back of the girl, hitched up her scraggy skirt, and climbed the three steps into the longhouse, where Zurotul's mother had given a final unmedicated pelvic push, expelling Zurotul, a mess of flesh, bone, membrane and bodily fluids.

It must be a disconcerting sight for a simple village woman—freshly out of labour, pain still searing, vagina gaping, sister having just disjointed the umbilical cord connecting her and her child—to see the village hag, whom everyone knew to trade capriciously in black magic, appear in view between her thighs from the vantage point on the floor. Following which, the demand of her newborn's placenta, which her husband handed over ingratiatingly, and the instantaneous consumption of this bloody gob that had been a hidden skin inside of her for three quarters of a year.

The smacking sound of the village hag's lips—recall that she was toothless—and the blood on her hands as she approached mother and newborn. Raising her hand, as the mother cringed, the words that fell from the village hag's lips:

She will be made for love.

Love Is No Big Truth

1.

There is no such thing in the world, as *I cannot live without you; you cannot live without me.* The earth spins. Time passes. Rice is eaten. What is there to disprove?

He left me a year after the accident that left my face misaligned. A public bus rammed into me, at the bus stop across the wet market. The cuts of chicken and vegetables in my red plastic bag fell to the ground, and the last thing I saw were the tomatoes rolling out onto the road, turning quickly into red pulp under car tyres.

When I woke up in the hospital after surgery, the first thing he said was, *Why were you so careless?*

And I knew that what he meant wasn't *I could have lost you.* What he meant was how much this would cost him, for the operation and the hospital stay.

2.

No, our generation, we don't do divorces. We're the make-do generation, the one that went through the war. We ate sweet potatoes three meals a day, and that was when we were lucky. When I told my daughter this years ago—she was complaining about my cooking, too bland—she said, If I had to eat sweet potatoes for three meals a day, I'd die.

So even when you can't make do any more—finally he said to me, I can't get off on *that*, referring to my misaligned face—what you do is to leave the surface intact, even as you tunnel far beneath the soil. He said it as if I were the one looking to be pleased sexually.

We're still legally married. He didn't even have the courtesy to move out, even when he brought her home. She was over the hill; heavy make-up over wrinkles, sparkly jersey over love handles, a Szechuan accent. He didn't have enough money to attract the younger ones. Anyway, he only managed to get her because that was the year he could get his savings out of his CPF.

I moved out in the end, to save myself and my daughter some face. That woman was hanging her soiled, lacy red bra and panty set in the common toilet. Drinking the tea I prepared. Using the chipped floral mug that was my daughter's.

3.

I wasn't.

He had been my only sexual partner. I don't know about him. I was only eighteen when we were married.

I never had an orgasm. It wasn't so irksome, before my menopause, sex. We saw it as part of a wife's duty to her husband—isn't it? Maybe because I've never had an orgasm, I won't understand. What you don't know, you can't crave.

No, I would never try to touch myself. No, it doesn't arouse my curiosity, not now at least. And before, I always saw it as something shameful—but we had to do it to carry on the line.

You had to do it for your husband. Always for someone else.

I'd never even held his hand. I don't know what was going on in my head, that first night. The only thing I remember: it hurt, but I didn't bleed. He was concerned—he asked me if I was sure I was a virgin, and I said, *Heavens, yes*. He wanted me to swear it on the honour of my family name and my mother's deceased soul. I wanted to slap him, but I swore instead, because if we were going to start it off on the wrong foot, it would be difficult to live together. Pride is not difficult to swallow when you weigh the odds. I've always been level-headed.

There was no such preparation. To pop out a baby the next year was something so unexpected, even after carrying it for nine months. Not knowing how to care for it. They say motherhood is instinctive. I think it's a lie. But repeat it long enough and all the women come to think it's true, come to be able to take care of this kicking, crying thing that came out of them.

We were watching a Hongkee movie called *Kangaroo Man* one weekend afternoon on TV, when my daughter was young. The lead character was carrying a baby to term in a pouch on his leg. When the plot became clear, my husband reached over for the remote and turned the TV off. I said, It's just a movie. He said it was disrespectful, that it would impart the wrong values to our daughter. We didn't argue. We just sat in silence and stared at the black screen for some time, all of us still thinking about the Kangaroo Man.

As an Asian wife you learn to hold your tongue. Your husband is always right—it isn't worth the fight. Sometimes, when I lost my head for just a bit and retorted, he would say, *Who puts the rice on the table? Shut the fuck up.* Perhaps it's different now that ladies hold down jobs as well. I don't know—is it any different?

4.

The last time I saw him was at our daughter's wedding. That was about five years ago—two years after the accident, a year after he left me. We sat together, because we'd not told anyone, much less the in-laws, about our estrangement—why make things difficult for your child? I'd rather suck it up, like a sponge over some lard grease.

We didn't speak to one another, only smiled congenially—if a little stiffly—in sync, at the relevant moments. His hairline had receded further, and when we were served shark's fin soup in small porcelain bowls, he started unscrewing something in his hands under the table. When everyone was making the most banter, he slid the bowl towards him and emptied the untouched soup into a small thermos.

I turned to him.

It's for her, he explained, coarse complexion reddening slightly. She wasn't happy I would be attending with you. Said I had to bring back the shark's fin.

As he stowed the thermos in his bag, I couldn't stop laughing. I'd never laughed so hard my whole life. I was always restrained, but something in me broke. Our in-laws turned towards me, bemused.

What's the joke? My daughter's father-in-law asked affably. He looked from my face to my husband's.

Men, I managed, through my laughter. *Women.*

When I got home, I lay down without removing my make-up or my banquet-going dress, and began sobbing. Was that bastard going soft with age? He would never have done something like that for me, not even in our salad days. But then again, we never had a courtship.

No, it wasn't jealousy, because jealousy is love and even then I was certain I had no more feelings for him—if I even had any to begin with. Companionship through time, I suppose, but not love, I don't think.

It was competitiveness.

Sport.

5.

We grew up on the same lane. We went to the same Chinese school, and we both stopped studying after Secondary Two, me to help out at home, him to tend to his father's vegetable store at the market. Neighbours, schoolmates, occasional playmates. This was the only reason why we got married—proximity and the elapsing of time—and this was a good reason in its time. Isn't that laughable? My uncle—whose care I came under after my parents died—said we'd spent too much time together, and that I was already devalued in the eyes of other prospective suitors.

The marriage was decided upon over a dim sum dinner downtown at which neither he nor I were present. Eating out at a restaurant was extravagant for kampung dwellers like us, but it was necessary: both sides wanted to show that they could afford it.

An almanac was consulted, a date set. My uncle and his father shook hands, as if sealing a favourable barter. If my mother had still been alive, the mothers might have smiled reservedly at each other, housework on both their minds: His mother: Now I'll have a daughter-in-law to clean the house. My mother: Now I'll have to clean the house on my own.

6.

There was no romance inherent.

And the funny thing was, the lack thereof didn't strike us as strange. When I say *us*, when I say *we*, I believe I speak for a good number of women my age. Go ask them.

Romance was only the stuff of the movies.

We paid fifty cents for this on a monthly basis, to see it transpire between Lin Dai and Kwan Shan on the big screen, weekly if we could afford it. We tied handkerchiefs to the seat to mark them as taken when we went outside to get kacang putih.

We never went with our husbands. We went on our own. It was female bonding more than anything else. We were separate beings, but we sighed at the same parts, laughed at the same parts, cried at the same parts. After the credits rolled, under the dim lights, you could seek out the gaze of another woman and find understanding there, and feel less alone.

I've never seen the world, never known anything else, everything I know is from the movies. This has been my solace, my self-betterment through the decades. From fifty cents to eight dollars, from kacang putih to popcorn. The year I turned fifty-five, joy: half-priced movie tickets for senior citizens. Once a year, I beg my daughter to help me with the computer, with the internet, to help me purchase a box set of one of my favourite directors. These box sets are my pride and joy. I dust them daily—Tsai Ming-Liang, Zhang Yi Mou, Hou Hsiao-Hsien. Sometimes, the shipping costs more than the box set, and I sit on the decision of the purchase for weeks. When I ask her to help me locate the item again, my daughter is very irritated. I save up for these box sets. I use only one square of toilet paper when I go to the bathroom. I walk back from the market rather than take the bus. Things add up.

I cry at almost everything I watch. Sometimes I feel like I'm not sure if I've truly grasped the movie, but it always teaches me something. I've learned so much from the movies, from eloquence to embitterment. Florid expressions of love and tragedy in the Chinese language, poetic monologues unseemly for a woman like me. The stall owners at the market rib me, half-jokingly, half-admiringly, say I speak like a woman of letters. I reply, in a jesting tone lest they think me proud, Who knows? The opportunities that were given to us in our day short-changed our destinies. Maybe you'd have been a philosopher, the vegetable stall woman says as she adds an extra carrot into my bag. Like Confucius. She's been giving me something extra ever since the accident—a tomato here, a carrot there, watercress. I want to tell her things add up. Confucius believed that women's place was below men's, I say. Our lot in this life, she says, shaking her head. Next life, I tell you, I want to be born a man.

7.

Do I feel alone now?

Every single day.

Not too long ago, I was trying to catch the eye of every older man around. At the void deck, at the supermarket, at the neighbourhood park. I wanted someone in my life again. After a long time, one day, someone looked back at me. The moment our eyes locked, I felt a deadweight tiredness in my bones. When he stood up from the park bench and walked towards me, I fled.

A relationship means exhaustion. Entrapment. I haven't the energy for the eventuality of it. Love is no big truth.

There was a point when I was lying down so much, I forgot to bathe for days. I forgot to eat. My daughter would come visit me—she stays with her in-laws, they have a terrace house—and she would fan her nose when she talked to me, asking me to eat the rice sets she'd bought. She started speaking to me in English, though we'd always spoken in Mandarin, though she knew I barely had a handful of English words. But always, in a few hours, she would leave. Even if I didn't eat, even if I didn't bathe.

After some time, I began bathing and eating whenever she came. Not to make her feel better, but to make myself feel better. Because if the situation were somehow reversed, I would never leave. I would make her better. They would have to rip me from her bedside.

I threw my bed away. Depression is easy when you have a bed.

I'm well now. The floor makes for good sleep.

8.

Does it seem curious now, that as a child, I thought you could die of a broken heart?

I'd never even seen my parents speak to one another, except at dinnertime. My mother would say, Dinner's ready. My father would grunt. Then we would eat. I thought my mother hated my father, but when he died, she jumped into his coffin.

It was the night of his funeral, whilst the priest was leading us through the rites. It took three uncles to pry her out of there. She left nail marks on the interior wood, and she smeared my father's make-up—the flesh-tone foundation the undertaker puts on, the lip colour.

My uncles found her in the river three days later. The word that went out was: here be a woman who loved her husband *that much*. The truth was probably that my mother had been so defined by the existence of my father that when he died, she couldn't see anything else before her.

She thought that she had to die with him. She knew nothing about Indian brides on funeral pyres. He'd closed his fist around her, she'd let him, and then when he died there was so much white space of possibility around her, she couldn't breathe.

9.

The first morning I woke on the floor, these words were in my head, as if someone had left me a note under the door in an anonymous hand: *loneliness is freedom.*

I wondered why I hadn't been turned on to this sooner.

I realised:

My daughter has completed her degree and gotten married, my husband has left me for a woman from mainland China. Finally, for once, I can do whatever I want. Maybe that, to you, sounds ridiculous. But your generation—the thing you are best at is placing yourselves first. You have no problems being your own person, even in relation to other people. It's as natural as breathing.

But for us, to have people in our lives, to have relations, is to have duties, is to serve. We can't shake it off. We can't be the ones to turn our backs. But when you are the one who has been left behind—the truth is that you have been set free.

I was independent of being a wife, a mother, even, a woman. I was simply, me. I felt an incredible elation course through my body. I went about my daily routines as if nothing had changed—and indeed, nothing *had* changed, but I knew that this was the start of something new, and that this something would last me through the end of my days.

You won't need it now, you are young and beautiful—beauty is subjective, but who would dispute that youth is beauty? But one day, it might be all that you need, so dig a hole and bury it like a bone, and don't say no one told you: *loneliness is freedom.*

Two Ways To Do This

ZUROTUL WAS MADE for love, only she was born in the wrong environs for love to occur.

Sometimes when the husband and wife were out, Zurotul would go to the wife's side of the wardrobe and pull out a dress or a pantsuit. Initially she only had enough nerve to hold the hanger up to her chin in the full-length mirror in the master bedroom, but finally she took to putting the garments on.

She progressed to lying on the wife's side of the bed, body turned towards where the husband would lie. Always she was careful to smooth out the bedclothes after, to redo her undoing of the morning's bed-making. Every morning when she made the bed, Zurotul would press her face into the husband's pillow. The faint smell of oil, dribbled saliva and something slightly milky.

When she prepared his meals, when she ironed his shirts and pants, when she laid out his socks across his work shoes and left them on the little stool by the door, she imagined them as spouses, she and him. These were, after all, spousal duties. It made her happy. She didn't need his touch. Once in a while, as he left the house, as he was locking up the gate, depending on where she stood, he would even call out *Bye!* to her, with that easy smile. She would look up from her sweeping or her wiping, heart a-flutter, to say: *Have a good day, Sir*. Those days were the best.

She took pride in taking good care of his dying mother, always cheerful and gentle to the shrivelled woman even though she was so far gone, coaxing her to swallow her medicine, turning her over by the hour to prevent bedsores, kneading moisturiser into her papery skin. The dying mother was asleep most of the time and hard of hearing, and she never once heard Zurotul calling her *ibu*, mother.

Zurotul was perfectly happy to have the husband in this way, if it weren't for the wife—the tantrums, the name-calling, the expectations of deference, all directed at the loving husband. It happened for any reason or no apparent reason at all, at least twice a week. The husband invisibly pummelled, you could see it in his face, but never seeming to tire. Yet even in his seeming tirelessness, she could feel him becoming smaller and smaller from being constantly chipped at. The man she loved was going under.

Then the day she saw the wife slap the husband, from the kitchen. The wife went off in a huff to the master bedroom and slammed the door shut. Zurotul ached. She poured a glass of water and approached the husband timidly. The husband was sitting on the sofa, his eyes red. When she proffered the glass of water, the husband dashed it away. The glass shattered on the terrazzo floor. Zurotul scurried for a rag to clean the mess and in her haste cut her hand on a glass shard. The husband heard her yelp and he took her hand in hers, applying pressure to stop the bleeding. I'm sorry, he was saying, I'm so sorry, it's just—

Zurotul began crying—the anxiety of having angered him, the empathy for this man, the fact of his touch, his hand on hers, how good it felt. He was half-holding her now, and she wished that it was after 10pm, which would've meant that she'd have had her daily shower: she wished she smelled better. She collected herself and, awkwardly, they came apart. He said he would go get her a plaster. As he rose to his feet, she saw that her blood was on his index finger. It was then that she remembered the village hag's dying words.

• • •

She'd always had irregular periods, and it was four months before she menstruated on the night of a full moon.

She served it to him the next morning, mixed into the instant coffee he had with his breakfast toast, further masked by a teaspoon of condensed milk. Zurotul had dipped in as much blood as she'd dared—with two fingers, back and forth, such that her nether regions were, likewise, greased with instant coffee.

She approached him shyly, ceremoniously, full of fear. Her hands shook as she brought him the cup. The wife looked at her quizzically, and it seemed for a moment Zurotul would be unable to set it down on the mahogany dining table.

Well? the wife said. Where's my jasmine green tea?

Coming, Ma'am, coming. Zurotul set the cup down and returned to the kitchen, turning to see if the husband had already taken a drink. Over time she'd noticed the angle at which he would reach for the cup, and she'd always made it a point to set the cup's handle down in a facilitative position. His eyes were on the morning paper and his hand was reaching for the cup. He drank and swallowed.

She spent the next week looking for signs. Once or twice she thought she noticed a new, marked displeasure in his tone to the wife, but nothing of consequence—he held his peace, gave in to the wife, and they went about their working lives. Zurotul was not overly disappointed. Much as she had believed in the mysticism of the hag, she might have been a crackpot after all, suffering the incoherent delirium of a tropical deathbed. Or perhaps, she'd performed the ritual wrongly—might it not be that instant coffee was an inappropriate base liquid? She knew, though, that she would never try again; it wasn't in her nature.

Almost exactly a month later, on a working day, the husband came home early. Sir, Zurotul said, early?

Sir not feeling well, he said, slipping off his shoes and socks. He went to his room and she hastened to the kitchen to make him a mug of warm water with honey and lemon.

She knocked on his door and he came to it, having stripped down to his boxers and the flimsy white singlet he would wear under his work shirt. He looked pale. She gave him the drink and he took it to his bed, lacing his fingers around the warm mug. She was kneeling to gather the fallen work shirt and pants by his bed, removing the leather belt from the belt loops, when she felt him behind her. He was hard.

Zurotul was clutching the laundry in her hands. They had the sour but powdery smell of perspiration dried off under office air-conditioning. Her heart was pounding. She wanted this to be special. She thought: *What would Ma'am not do?*

Without turning round to face him she pulled her shorts and underwear down, offering him the tawny warmth within, then prostrated herself on the floor, her face in his soiled office wear. He took her again, and again, and again.

• • •

He started coming home during his lunch breaks, as often as he could. She took to waiting for his silver Toyota to pull into the HDB car park at half past noon. She loved watching the husband step out of the car and point the remote lock to it. Sometimes if the neighbourhood was quiet she could hear the Toyota's locking beep.

He preferred it on the floor, from the back. This, too, was her preference—the one time he'd slipped under her, she felt a lack of confidence as she sat astride him. She thought it felt wrong, being able to watch his face lose control to the pleasure she was giving him from above. They fucked in every room in the house—from the living room to the study—besides the room where the dying mother slept. For a treat, they would do it in the master bedroom's en suite bathtub, and then take a shower together. She loved holding on to his penis and scrubbing it with her hands, the way she would a radish or a carrot. She would smile to herself when she prepared root vegetables. They never talked before or after sex, but she thought he seemed relaxed and happy with her.

When he was away and she'd finished the housework, she would read the labels of the toiletries in the master bathroom, opening the caps up and placing her nose to them. *Cranberry Body Scrub. Mint & Jojoba Conditioner. Brazil Nut Moisturiser.* The words looked so exquisite though she didn't know what they meant.

They began to have perpetually bruised knees. They began wearing clothing that would cover their knees—he now slept in pyjama pants rather than sport shorts. The wife never noticed. She continued with her tantrums and the husband continued giving in, though he now did so in an ever-so-slightly ironic way.

• • •

As all things go, there came the day when the wife returned to the apartment at lunch time to pick up a dossier she'd left on the bedroom table.

As it was, they were having sex in the shower. They'd never had to stifle their cries for the bedridden mother was hard of hearing anyway. The wife heard the running water, the moaning. She opened the bathroom door. Her husband, her maid, down on their knees in the tub, jets of running water from the shower hose falling upon them.

The wife screamed, *The maid? You really couldn't do any better?* She turned away and stalked out of the room.

The husband was trembling. He grabbed a towel and ran after her, out the house, wet.

Zurotul remained under the running water, hugging her naked body for a long time.

• • •

She was to be repatriated. She didn't qualify as a transfer maid because of what had happened. She was a loose, dangerous woman—unsuited to be a domestic helper. She sat in the back room of Happy Maid Employment Services Pte Ltd.

Somehow, she'd imagined that if they were ever found out, he would choose her—how could he not? She kept his house clean, she took care of his mother, she cooked his favourite dishes, she gave him pleasure. He would be crazy not to choose her.

It surprised her, too, that the wife had opted to stay. Perhaps she would excoriate the husband and pay him back in his own coin, slow burn.

But I love Sir long time, she'd said repeatedly, blubbering, but I love Sir long time.

The wife got up and slapped her smartly across the face. Love? The wife gave a bark of laughter. What do *you* think you know about love?

• • •

It was a five-hour bus ride from the airport, and a three-hour walk in from where the bus stopped. She was careful to avoid the main paths that were used by the villagers. She could feel the forest teeming with wildlife as she stepped through it. She realised she'd missed this, whilst in the city. Finally she found the old shack, dank and caved in.

In the shack, there was a dirty jar of dried areca nuts in a corner of a hand-hewn shelf, cobbled together with large branches and stones. Zurotul unscrewed the lid, sprinkled a handful into her mouth and started chewing, as she perused the contents of the other jars—dead spiders, shards of glass, various lengths of rope, and one that was obscured by fungi. There was a ragged robe hung on a nail in a corner of the shack, and Zurotul found herself removing her polo t-shirt, cheap jeans and shoes, and putting the robe on.

Clearing away weeds and roots from the area before the shack, she found the large beige rock she'd used to mark the village hag's resting place. She'd dug the grave with her bare hands, and evidently it had not been deep enough—she saw a white bone, perhaps a rib, protruding from the soil amidst the undergrowth. Again she felt the butterfly sensation in her lower abdomen, and this time she rested a hand on it. She'd swallowed back her vomit the week in transit at the agency every morning, afraid any sign would give it away, that they would make her abort the unborn child who'd only just begun to be substantially enough formed to tease her womb. She knew it was a girl she carried. She reached out and stroked the bleached bone gently, and made her first prayer for her daughter:

She will be made for love.

Alice, You Must Be the Fulcrum of Your Own Universe

WE'RE IN THE Flyer, the one meant to trump the London Eye as the tallest observation wheel in the world, and she's started to hyperventilate. Each ride, each oscillation takes half an hour, and I look at her small, thin frame, her bony shoulders, her prominent cheekbones, and I wonder if there is enough breath inside her to hyperventilate for half an hour and come out intact.

We don't have a plastic bag on us, but I do know I have to find some way to restrict her airflow, so I end up putting my mouth over hers.

She breathes through me, breathes me in, breathes me out, and her sharp intakes of breath slow gradually. When she catches her breath, she says lightly: *The last time I was kissed for that long, I was eighteen, under a banyan tree.* Bad joke, I say. Do you need a doctor? We stand by the glass windows of the capsule and look out at the bay.

Do you know that right under Marina Bay is a cesspool? The waste can't flow out to sea any more. If you fall in, you need a tetanus jab.

• • •

She keeps doing this, taking me to places high above ground.

First, it was the cable cars near the port, a thing of my 80s childhood, then the Flyer by the bay, then the hyper-modern infinity pool on the fiftieth floor of the grandest hotel in town with the basement casino, for which you had to be a hotel guest to enter. Her niece and her family, who lived in London, were staying in that hotel and she was taking them around, but she'd deposited them at Orchard Road for the day and she had the spare pass key—would I like to go to the pool with her?

If you're feeling lucky, we could go play roulette after.

She was in a fluffy white bathrobe, as was I. My swimsuit was well worn; when I put it on I realised that it had thinned out in some unfortunate regions. I hadn't swum in years. I wagered with myself on the cut of her swimsuit. And what sort of swimsuit would I wear when I was sixty-six? The answer was clear, which was that I could never imagine myself as the kind of old lady who would swim.

We got to the deck, and she unfastened and dropped her robe in one economical movement. Her swimsuit was a simple black one piece, turtle-necked, cut in at the shoulders. I'd expected looser skin, but her flesh tone was not too uneven. She turned to me, and I fumbled with the belt of the plush robe.

We slid into the large pool that overlooked the city, that appeared to merge with the horizon. We stared out at the city, at the monumental greenhouses by the bay, rising like a quicksilver beast from land that used to be sea.

Does the city ever frighten you?

Not ever.

How do you know what I'm asking?

Because I can smell your fear. Not me. I love change.

Is that why you're beautiful? If you keep up with the times, the times go gentler on you because there's less catching up to do?

She laughed, chlorinated hand held up to her crimson mouth—who wears lipstick into a pool?

I like the thought. Now tell me, have you ever pantomimed a picnic across a swimming pool floor?

• • •

We were two strangers standing outside the UK embassy, a steady rain falling beyond the shelter of the eaves, unequipped with umbrellas. She unclasped her hexagonal white leather handbag and brought out a cigarette case.

You're going to the United Kingdom?

To study in London, yes, in September.

Oh, I'll be there in October, to visit my niece for a month. Perhaps I'll bump into you outside Harrods or something, wouldn't that be funny. What will you study?

Art. At Central Saint Martins.

Ah, an artist, she said conspiratorially, placing the cigarette to her lips. *I read law at Oxford when I was your age, but I've always admired artists.* She lit up with a mother-of-pearl lighter, her head tilted at an angle to catch the flame.

I'm Jennifer, she said as she exhaled, *but please call me Jenny.*

Auntie Jenny.

No. Just Jenny.

Jenny.

We stood there talking for a long time. When the rain stopped, we traded numbers.

• • •

Jenny laughs with her hand over her mouth and uses words like *deportment, haberdashery, cavalier*. Men thirty, forty years younger than her hold doors open for us when we're out, and she winks at them. She takes my hand on the street and we walk for hours, fingers laced. I get tired before she does.

How many lovers have you had? she asks me in a café. She's wearing a smart black hat, as if she were going to the races. None yet, I say, and she laughs. And you? *Oh my, they're innumerable*, Jenny says as she asks for more sugar syrup for her iced tea. You're married, aren't you, I say, and she says, *Sure I am—but no children. Tied my tubes when I was thirty and my mother-in-law almost had a fit.* She looks at me and says as she puts down her teacup, *It's important to live for yourself. To know life.*

I'm draining the tea in my cup, and she's looking at me expectantly. When I say nothing, she leans forward and asks, *What are you afraid of?* I stare at the street outside for a long time, but she is patient. I'm afraid of giving myself away, because I don't know what I am yet, I say finally. Jenny puts a hand on my knee as if she knows something about me I don't know about myself. She finishes up her éclair and then she says, *You don't have to be afraid to give, because we are always in a process of becoming.* She wipes a spot of cream from the side of her mouth, licks her finger. *Alice, you must be the fulcrum of your own universe.*

On the weekdays I don't see her, I think of her cheeks falling in when she chain smokes, the slight frown before she exhales, the way she teases me out of myself. The thrill of stepping out of the conversation to find myself less guarded. Are you doing charity? my mother began asking me. She'd found it sweet until we began seeing each other every weekend. Does she see you as her granddaughter? my mother wants to know, and I think of Jenny's mother-of-pearl lighter, her painted nails and the ropy veins on the backs of her hands. We're friends, I say. Friends? Yes, friends. You don't even see Mama once a month, and don't you have friends your age? Mama only speaks Teochew, I can't even understand her, and besides, Jenny's different. My mother pauses. Is she rich? Maybe she'll include you in her will.

• • •

Jenny, I can't see you so much any more.

Why not?

I can't cheat on her.

Cheat? On who?

My grandmother.

She laughs. *Why do you look at it that way? I won't deny I took a shine to you at first sight though.*

It won't do for you to tell me things like that.

Why not?

I wish you were my grandmother.

Silly girl. If I were your grandmother, things would be different. Why spoil a good thing?

• • •

We're seated by the pier. She's reading by the dying sunlight, and I'm sketching her in charcoal. I ask, Don't you have to be home? We're both wearing shades, but even so she doesn't look at me when she answers. Her neck trembles under a silk scarf—little accoutrements for all the wrinkles she's eager to hide from me.

I'm not ten, she says.

Yeah, but you're not thirty either, I say.

She turns to me and smiles indulgently, as if she finds the remark charming. We're trying to look past our dark lenses into each other's eyes.

So it's all downhill from here, back to curfew and responsible relationships, then on to liquid food and adult diapers?

Yes. I'll see you home? Your husband will worry if you don't join him for dinner.

My husband can ladle his own rice and pick from the dishes. It's all laid out on the table. I did it before I headed out.

He's used to being served, isn't he?

Being used to something is such a poor excuse for prolonging anything, but it seems a national pastime, don't you think? We let ourselves get into the habit of the grind, we let the grind wear us down.

But isn't it cause and effect?

It is, but only if we look at things linearly—everyone does—but life isn't so simple, is it?

You know, Jenny, I think I'm not going to marry.

Because of all the shit I've been telling you?

No. Because at the tail end of all the shit I would just give up. I wouldn't be able to meet somebody like me when I was sixty-six, hold onto them like a giant lobster, and have them enjoy my grip. I'd just watch them slide right past me.

She knows this is marvel, not insult. She knows I'm complimenting her, and not myself. We look out at the lake and she reclines on me, into me, as if I'm a familiar canoe. Her shoulder blades press lightly on my breasts. She smells nothing like an old lady. I tell myself I will forever remember how important this is, to smell nothing like an old lady when I am an old lady.

The sun goes down and we rise to leave.

• • •

Alice? I think I'm a little in love with you. It isn't your fault.

What sort of love is this?

I have no idea.

If you do this, Jenny, I can't see you any more.

Why not?

I thought I was safe with you. You're betraying my trust.

What?

I thought I could be myself around you, and nothing would happen.

I'm telling you my feelings, and you're making it about yourself.

Aren't your feelings about me?

• • •

She's walking towards me with a Singapore Sling in each hand; she's said to meet in the bar of Raffles Hotel. It's late afternoon and the only people who meet in bars in the afternoons are in the movies, but it comes so naturally to her, in her nude pantyhose and cream pumps and apricot dress, salmon lipstick. She's always about trying something new, something she's never done before, something I've never done before, or best yet, something we've both never done before.

I'm never allowed to pay for anything, I've stopped trying. She adjusts herself on the bar stool, with decorum, and hands me the glass. I avoid the maraschino cherry, while she pops it into her mouth, and raises her glass. She plucks the decorative fuchsia paper umbrella from her drink and slots it behind her ear, into her hair. We clink glasses, and she withdraws from her handbag an envelope.

Will you go away with me? Nothing fancy, just a weekend in Penang. We sold the land, they're tearing my childhood home down. I want to see it a last time, and I would love for you to come with me.

I open my mouth, but she speaks again.

If the dates don't suit you or you don't want to, it's fine—I just went ahead and got tickets first, you know how I am—I don't want you to think I was being presumptuous.

• • •

We're in Penang and she's holding the keys to a rented manual car, khaki-coloured with faded blue suede seats.

What's your dialect group?

Teochew.

Ga gi nang, she exclaims, pleased.

What's that?

She looks at me and clucks her tongue.

Now look here, can't you speak a word of Teochew? Look at me, I speak beautiful English, but also Chinese, Teochew, Shanghainese and Cantonese.

Lucky you.

She softens: *It means 'our own people'.*

That's really old-fashioned.

How do you mean?

It cancels out other people.

It does, but I'm happy to be closer to you. It's what we do as human beings. Cancel and see what's left standing.

We slide into the car. Jenny adjusts the rear-view mirror and I buckle up.

When you're at school, can I come visit? I'll be at my niece's anyway. We could go for tea, jam on scones and all. We could go see Rembrandts and Vermeers and what-nots.

Of course we can.

You won't be too busy for me? She asks suddenly, putting a hand to her neck, then drawing the seatbelt across her torso.

I'll always have time for you, Jenny.

That's what you say now, she says, smiling as she revs the engine. *Let me take you somewhere?*

Anywhere, Jenny, I say. I love saying her name.

Even to the end of time? She's smiling slyly now, her eyes bright.

Now you're being cheesy.

She releases the clutch and I roll the windows down, her set-perm flying in the wind.

• • •

We climb the low gate, I help her over. She's more than sprightly for an old lady; she's limber, in the way that makes you want to touch. She's shed her age along the way, hair unloosed from its low chignon, hands and wrists unencumbered by her rings and bracelets. Her body is in a loose-fitting shift, and she's left her shoes in the car, she says she wants to feel the floorboards beneath her bare feet. Her bunions make me want to learn to love her more.

We're back in her ancestral home, and she wanders in with a lilting step so light it would seem she was sixteen.

This is where my sister hid when she was sad. This is where my father caned my brother. This is where I sat by the feet of my mother as she braided my hair.

We go up the stairs with its rotting banister. I walk behind her, watching the backs of her feet, the tendons of her Achilles heels. *This is my bedroom,* she says. It still has a vanity desk with an old mirror on it, and a termite-bitten bed frame. I imagine her as a girl, in cotton nightclothes, lying in bed.

We return later in the afternoon, fed on assam laksa and kueh tutu, and then it is just a construction site. We let the piler come in. We watch as the ground is shot through with holes. We hear the crash of walls being pulled down. She startles as the heavy drill hits the concrete, her old lady body against me, flimsy as a kitten.

• • •

She'd picked me up in a cab on our way up to the airport, but on the leg back, after clearing immigration, as we walk out of the departure hall, she tells me her husband is picking her up, would I like a lift home? Before I can answer she's waving to a neatly dressed old man leaning against an old, boxy Mercedes Benz. He walks towards us and she slips a hand into my skirt pocket. He relieves her of her hand luggage.

He nods to me. She says: *This is the girl I've been talking about.*

Ah, he says, my missus has told me so much about you. I hope she hasn't been a bother? A young girl like you has surely got the world on her plate like an oyster.

Oh no, not at all. I enjoy Jenny's company. She says the strangest things.

Then you must be a little strangelette yourself.

They begin a small domestic conversation: How was his appointment with Dr Wong? She won't be cooking beans any more since his gout has returned. Dinner will be delayed because when they get home she needs to set the chicken out to thaw. He misses her black fungus chicken. There's a fleck of something at the corner of her mouth and he extends his hand quite unconsciously to flick it gently away. She touches the spot. I realise there and then that I know nothing about love.

Can I offer you a lift home?

No, I'll just take the bus home, thank you.

She doesn't live that far from our place, Jenny says.

Don't stand on ceremony, he says, plus you've got luggage.

It's a straight bus, and this is just a duffel.

Jenny gives me a look. I avoid her gaze. Her husband says kindly, All right, you take care then. I'm sure we'll meet again.

Jenny says: *But I insist.*

Jen, her husband says, let the girl do as she wants. Aside, to me, Don't mind her, she's used to getting her way. I've known her since she was sixteen and she's never changed one bit. I let her have her way all the time but sometimes she doesn't remember that not everyone is in love with her. He chuckles affectionately, holds out a hand to her.

Jenny is offended. She walks away. He excuses himself, catches up with her, puts his palm on the small of her back. I don't wait to see them slip into the car.

I take the bus home. The afternoon sun blazes through the glass and burns one side of my face.

• • •

I don't take her calls.

She appears on my doorstep, says, *You haven't been taking my calls.*

Your husband, I say. I cross my arms, then realise I am crossing my arms, and uncross them.

My husband what?

Your husband is a perfect gentleman. The two of you have a good thing going on.

I never said there was anything wrong between us.

Then—

I told you I didn't know what manner of love this was, this love I have for you. But surely you weren't thinking of it as romance?

I choke on my own tongue, a coughing fit ensues, she pats me on the back as if our ages are reversed. As I am fighting for air, even before the cough ceases, I begin speaking in between each hack before the words leave me:

I guess I thought there was a big hole in your life, and that hole was in the shape of me.

She stops patting my back. I stop coughing.

I thought you were in need. But it was greed.

We regard each other as wary animals might, circling without once moving.

What the hell, she says finally. *You're not social services. I'm not a case file. What does it matter?*

It's sort of like the difference between love and lust.

Don't namedrop things you know nothing about.

I never want to see you again.

Don't say that—you don't mean it.

I'll buy you a rocking chair. Isn't that enough for women your age? Knitting needles, a ball of yarn? Why do you think you're entitled to attention and devotion? You've overstayed your welcome.

You can't leave now.

Why do you think everyone is supposed to yield to you?

Because I'm old, and I'm dying.

You're not dying.

We're all dying.

If you die, I will be relieved.

I dare you to say that again.

If you die, I will be relieved.

I never want to see you again.

Perfect. Didn't I say that just a minute ago?

She turns sharply and crosses the lawn, gets into her car.

There is a spilt feeling inside of me, rising in my chest, as her car turns the corner.

• • •

We were on that pier when I put down my charcoal stick and asked her: Jenny, is life difficult or easy?

Life is difficult. That is the way it was designed.

Why was it designed this way?

Life is difficult because in order to progress we have to come to terms with the things we do not have.

She'd looked at me from under her shades, over her book.

But life is so easy, with you. Who needs progress?

Jenny!

What?

You can't tell people things like that.

Says who? I just did.

• • •

In London, sometimes, I wonder if she is here too, as I ride the Tube from Waterloo to King's Cross, as I read a book in Regent's Park, as I encounter the golden figure kneeling by the lake in Dalí's *Metamorphosis of Narcissus* at Tate Modern. I try hard to be unafraid, to know life, to give, to receive the city as it opens up to me. I go partying with my classmates. I fellate a Welsh boy in a pub alley one night, and for a few dark hours I feel worldly, smug, and then when I wake up I can't eat for the week after without remembering the sickening mineral taste of him or the way he kept pushing on the back of my head or the fact that I can't even remember his name. I think of Jenny, her hand on my knee, saying *Alice, you must be the fulcrum of your own universe*, and I feel the shame in my chest, that I can only pivot around people.

Penny for your thoughts? my date, a long-limbed boy with light freckles, asks as we gaze at *Metamorphosis of Narcissus*. I look at his face and see that he thinks we're going to talk about the Surrealist Manifesto, that particular shade of blue Dalí was so partial to, or how Dalí accused Joseph Cornell of stealing his dreams.

I was just thinking of someone I used to know.

A boy back in Singapore?

No, a woman.

I didn't know you swing both ways.

I don't. She's old enough to be my grandmother.

• • •

Back after half a year for Chinese New Year, I decide to go by her house after a week. I've been thinking about the crinkles around her eyes when she smiles. Those colourless lips and the witticisms they issue, her paper-thin skin. The veins in her temple, the white roots of her dyed hair, and that rich, rich smell.

My mother makes me take two pairs of oranges to pay my festive respects. Jenny's not the type, I say, but she presses them into my hands.

The house is boarded up, fenced in by blue construction tarpaulin. There's a construction notice tacked to the gate: LOT OF TWO DETACHED HOUSES WITH BASEMENT AND SWIMMING POOL. I should have called, besides that I'd cancelled my local line before I left. It'd felt good leaving no trace, she wasn't young enough to know how to track me down on the internet.

I ring the neighbour's bell, and a plump woman answers it. Hello, I'm a friend of Jenny's. Do you happen to know where they moved to? She looks at me uncertainly. Well, Charles lives with his nephew now. Jennifer—surely you've heard about Jennifer? I've been abroad, I say. I feel the blood leaving my face and I bite down on my tongue, just enough for it to smart. She looks inwards at her living room, where her relatives have halted a game of cards, waiting for her to return. There goes my gambling luck, she mutters as she turns back to me. Bone cancer, she says, stage four. Frightening to see her at the end, so tiny and frail. And Charles—well, imagine the heartbreak. The funeral, just last month, and then Charles sold off the place. For a grand sum, I might add. Property market is red-hot now, and it wouldn't do an old man any good to live alone in a house so big, would it?

• • •

I go around in my parka in London, putting my hood up, and the smallest things remind me of her. Sugar cubes. Pantyhose. Cigarette smoke. Revolving doors. Perfume with rose notes. Always, I try never to pause. Still I imagine her lowering her shades, smiling at me, just me, saying, *Don't look back into the sun*, and then I find myself crying in a café or on a sidewalk or in a record store again, and over the speakers I hear Paul McCartney's voice singing 'All You Need Is Love', and the *pa-pa-rum-pa-rum* flourish of trumpets.

She was singing in the hotel shower in Penang. The bathroom door was shut, but lying on the bed, I could hear her. The bed was a double. She was singing a medley of Beatles choruses, but she'd changed all the lyrics. She had the voice of a woman who'd smoked a thousand cigarettes.

She came out singing 'All You Need Is Love', only, she'd changed the lyrics to 'All You Need Is Love Is A Lie'. She was smiling at me as she sang, and I at her. She sat in front of the mirror, brushing her hair out. When she went back in to the bathroom to wash up, I walked over to the dresser, placed the hairbrush to my nose, and breathed her in.

I went back to bed, reclining into the pillows. I heard her gargling, spitting, gargling, spitting. I heard the rindle of water as she washed her face, the small splashes. I heard her put the toilet seat cover down. I heard her peeing. Listening to her peeing as I lay on the hotel bed, my heart was fit to burst.

Fourteen Entries from the Diary of Maria Hertogh

30th December 1950

I am only thirteen but I would like to tell you something: there is something far worse than not being loved by anybody, and that is being loved by *everybody*.

28th March 1951

Have you heard of Helen of Troy, i.e. *Sweet Helen/the face that launched a thousand ships?*

Today, Sister Ana read me a poem about her. In Plutarchian poetry it sounds guileless enough, but these ships were warships and men died, empires fell.

My name—my secret name, my real name—is Nadra, and last year, men on a small island in Malaya rioted over me. Muslims from Pakistan, Saudi Arabia and Indonesia volunteered to send my Ibu money to pay for lawyers and to rally demonstrators. I am not that beautiful though I do have curly brown hair and my skin is white. I mention this because on that island, they had yellow or brown or black skin, and dark hair. Here they tell me my name is Huberdina Maria Hertogh, or Bertha. My hair was once blonde but when I was seven my Ibu—in fear that I would be taken away by the Japanese if they knew I was a European child—shaved my head and applied candlenut oil to my scalp for a year, till the roots grew out dark.

As I write this, I am thinking of how to best upset Adeline, my so-called birth mother. She has taken me from Ibu, with the full weight of the Netherlands behind her. The truth is that she gave me up to Ibu when I was six, along with an old sewing machine. What she is saying now is that she only meant to put me in Ibu's care for three days, and that she didn't manage to fetch me back because she was interred by the Japanese. I do not believe her for a minute.

I write this diary in solidarity with the likes of Anne Frank, whom Sister Ana told me about. One day I will die, having suffered, and someone shall find my words worthwhile. Like Anne, I live in an attic, shrouded in a certain type of secrecy, though I sleep between my two sisters. They are afraid I will attempt to run away. You must forgive me the indulgent alignments with great women of beauty or composure long gone.

Alone here I find myself yearning for an abstracted comfort—certainly not from the bosom of Adeline, who mostly thinks to pick on me, who makes me perform the chores of the entire household. Though she sometimes furnishes me with rice for my meals—the grainy bread and potatoes they have for three meals are so disagreeable—she has already wrought onto me violence, and I shall never forgive her.

3rd April 1951

Allahu Akbar.

Allah, I beg your forgiveness.

I know you've long seen the photograph they took of me, the one headlined *Bertha knelt before Virgin Mary statue*, and also the one on the front page of the *Singapore Standard*, where I held hands with the Reverend Mother. To tell the truth, it was the Reverend Mother who took my hands in hers. I merely thought it rude to pull away. I was laughing in the photograph by the piano, because the nuns had made jokes with me right before the photograph was taken. They might as well have held me down and tickled me. Understand, the nuns were kind, but I knew my allegiance even amidst this kindness. They were gentle as they took away my baju kurung and gave me a Western dress. They brushed my hair and put a big maroon bow in my hair: *There, there. How pretty you look now, Bertha!*

But Allah, I answer only to your name.

I still make ablution here. In secret, you understand. I have in the cramped attic I share with my sisters a saucer that they believe is for the cat, but when it is quiet I perform wudhu, wetting hands, mouth, nose, arms, face, running my damp hands through my hair.

Each day I make the same prayer: I pray that those who died because of me and the hundreds who were injured might forgive me, be they Malay, Chinese, Indian, European or Eurasian. Will you widen your embrace to bring your grace to these souls?

I remember the ways of prayer Ibu taught me. I found on a world map Saudi Arabia, where Mecca is. The Netherlands is atop it and leftward, so in my room I kneel to the diagonal right to face the Ka'ba.

Allah, I pray you will keep Ibu and Mansoor safe and warm, that we may be reunited soon.

17th May 1951

Today I said to Adeline, It is obvious you do not love me. That was why you handed me to someone else. Why did you come and take me back?

Adeline said, At that time, I did not have the means to take care of all the children.

I said, if you could feed six children, surely it was possible that you could take care of seven. Besides, I do not eat that much.

Here, Adrianus struck me. He said: You ungrateful child. The exact words of the Dutch Commissioner upon my arrival at the Schiphol airport on 15th December last year, when he extended his hand in greeting right before the press conference and I refused to shake it. Why would I?

The thousands of people shouting my name in the sub-zero winter on the tarmac. Yet more people upon our arrival at Bergen-Op-Zoom. The car had to stop half a kilometre away from the house because of the people crowded around. Someone said they'd been camping here since dawn, for my arrival, could they touch my face? They reached out their hands, and when I recoiled, they flinched. How incredible it is, to mistake your selfishness as someone else's happiness.

2nd December 1951

Whilst doing the laundry today, my hands bled. I had been wondering when they would. Being unable to feel them any more, pain is barely a good indication, what with the blisters.

The water has turned to ice and still I am made to rinse the clothes by hand—the clothes of the entire family: Adeline, Adrianus, Wiesje, Corry, Kees, Benny, Carol and Ria. How I should like to rip up Adrianus's workpants or Ria's apron.

As the skin of my wet hands shrunk up, I thought of Adeline's claim to the court in Singapore that Ibu was a babu who had kidnapped me and taken me to the jungle. The jungle! Ibu's houses in Bandung and Malaya were finer than this one in Bergen-Op-Zoom. In Bandung, we had a maid and a gardener. Here I am, a babu indeed, mopping all the floors and making all the beds.

My Ibu was many things, but not a babu. A Japanese language teacher and a jeweller, for example. She would give me jewellery of the latest fashions and I would play like I was Mata Hari. I was the envy of all the children of the village. Later, Adeline took away all the jewellery Ibu had given to me. The small freshwater pearl earrings I wore are now on her earlobes.

29th March 1952

I am already fifteen but I go to grade school in the poor company of girls five years younger at St Gerardus Majella, because I have only recently been schooled in Dutch. They are quick, as girls are, to stick together and to play petty games and to call outsiders names.

They call me *reus*, which means giant. It does not bother me awfully—I have always been called names, they called me orang puteh, orang puteh, for my fair complexion back then—but I am sad that I have no one to speak with in Malay, here. I fear the words are slipping away from me, and so it gives me great comfort to be penning these words, in this diary, in the tongue of my Malayan motherland.

We are forbidden to speak Malay at home, although all of us but Ria, who was born in the Netherlands, know it, having lived in Malaya. In a fit of anger last week I'd said to Corry—Aku hati jahat. Adeline was beside herself and told me to mop the floors, knowing I'd already done it. Adeline is herself Eurasian—her mother, my grandmother, Nor Louise, was a bangsawan actress. Uncle Soewaldi, her brother, was Muslim, and married an Indonesian woman—though Adeline lied about this in court.

She'd placed her hand on the Bible, the book she so reveres, and swore to the judge and the courtroom that she would tell the truth, the whole truth, and only the truth. Now she makes me sit by her knee as she reads Psalms.

15th December 1953

Ibu, the last thing I heard you say to me, that I said back to you, word for word, was this:

I would rather kill myself than be separated from you.

Then you fainted dead away, and they took me with them in the car.

It has been three years now, and we are both still alive.

We disappoint each other.

27th April 1956

Only a week into this marriage and I begin to wonder if this was a poor choice—choosing a husband to lose a mother. Surely no one else thinks this way? I wake in the morning to the way Gerard's mouth trembles when he snores, how he hugs his hands to his chest and it makes me feel dull and clumsy—a bad start to the day. At least at Adeline's I had my own bed to myself: I only had to put up with her wheedling in the day, and I could easily pack a lunch and eat it by the canal.

I read today of the bones of an ancient anchoress found in the Getrudiskerk. The anchoress was sealed in a space between the church's walls to anchor the church from evil. Before she was sealed into the cell, a ritual was performed on her, not unlike the Last Rites. All she had with her was a Bible, a chamber pot and a brick-sized hole that opened up to street-level. The faithful would leave her food scraps and drinks of water, and help to clear her slops. If their faith waned or if they were merely forgetful, the anchoress would easily suffer—or die from—thirst and starvation.

Would that I could be such a woman, if only to get away. From mothers; from men. From childbearing; from caprice.

15th February 1957

The birth of a fat baby boy, mine. Adeline is very happy. I saw her standing red-faced with excitement through the course of my labour, as if it were the veritable beginning of her deliverance. As if through *my* own motherhood *she* would be cleansed—that I would now finally understand what she'd meant every time she said she did it for my own good. That it would become the truth.

We have named him Frans.

2nd July 1967

Frans, Marlies, Theo, Huub, Carolien, Paul, Maryolien, Hans, Peter, Silvija.

Every year a baby, as if by clockwork. I am constantly pregnant. I am more pregnant than not pregnant in a year every year for the past ten years, and I realise this to be, perhaps, the true destiny of a married woman of my times. Which is not unlike, say, that of a sow.

18th January 1976

A young woman came to Het Pumpke today. She had cropped hair and she wore jeans. She walked straight up to me—I had my hands full of crockery from tidying a table—and introduced herself as a graduate student of feminist and post-colonial theory at Erasmus up in Rotterdam. Gerard eyed her carefully. She said she was writing a paper on me as a pawn of symbolism for the last vestiges of the perception of pride for a vacating colonial power. I remember this clearly enough to write it down word for word because I asked her to repeat this three times—there were so many big words and she said them in a single breath each time. She said it as if I were supposed to be honoured, but I could forgive her yet, because she was not working for the media, and because her eyes were bright with that youthful determination.

What does that have to do with me, I asked, and she thought I was dull, that I had not kept up and she would have to re-explain herself.

You are my thesis, she kept saying.

I understand, I said again. But what does your thesis have to do with me?

This time I think she understood. She sat down and ordered up some *stamppot*. I continued busying myself with the cafeteria. She looked out the window and smoked some cigarettes. The way she put out her cigarettes was decisive and harsh, the way a man would.

Finally at closing time she approached me and said: Your life was not your own.

I was not expecting this. Yes, I said and then I cried. I lifted my apron to wipe my face, and she tried to embrace me.

Please, I said, please leave me alone. She hesitated, then walked out, leaving a tip on the counter. It was a big tip—twenty guilders. I saved it up to pay for my Maryolien's treatment for pneumonia.

31st January 1987

They say this resort was once owned by Frank Sinatra, that Marilyn Monroe spent a winter vacation here in Lake Tahoe. It's thoughts like these I try to hold onto when I am fishing used condoms out of WCs, even if I'm in the small motel across the boulevard, where Marilyn would never be. To make ends meet, I work in seven chalets and motels. I don't give myself rest days. What is that line? An idle mind is the devil's playground?

One of the first few English words I learned was *chambermaid.* Also, *the land of the free*—something that Ben said to me, over and over, like a charm—and *prostitution.* It surprised me that *prostitution* was not legal in the rest of the forty-nine states of *the land of the free*—only in regulated brothels in Nevada. Back in the Netherlands we have no hang-ups such as these, as long as they are consenting adults.

Whenever I think of this term—*consenting adults*—I think of Mansoor. How amusing it is that we were parted because I was—by the British Constitution—only a child. One year shy of my fourteenth birthday—the lawful age for a Muslim marriage, three years shy of being sixteen, the legal matrimonial age in England. Amusing because if what they feared was the untoward behaviour of a husband nine years my senior, they were guided by their own poor moral standards, not Mansoor's. It was Mansoor who suggested to Ibu we should have a nikah gantung, because I was young and he was still a trainee teacher. He said we would consummate our marriage when I was twenty-one. He would have been thirty then. He would have waited for my maidenhead for eight years.

Three divorces later, never again have I experienced such gentility in a man. What they want right off the bat is the old in-out. The sooner the better. To think that the word that went around was that my Muslim husband was a savage, whom I needed protection from, when he was in fact descended from a family of nobility, just like Ibu, and more educated than any other man I have been with since. *De Telegraaf* published our wedding photograph and called me The Child Bride. Mansoor wore his round spectacles that, to me, gave him his scholarly air, and his songkok, grinning broadly for the camera. A girl from my school told me once: I saw your wedding photograph the year before you returned. My father showed it to me and my sisters. Everyone was very angry that you were marrying a monkey.

My Malay husband was the finest man I ever met, I retorted, and she couldn't tell if I was joking. We were only fifteen then, and had had limited contact with men—but it has been true—I mean it till this day: Mansoor is the finest man I have ever met.

23 March 1988

In the chalets and motels of Lake Tahoe, at any time of the day, couples are always being intimate with one another. I work both the morning and night shift. In the cheaper motels where the walls are thinner, I hear them loud and clear as the foghorn signals in the harbour.

Whenever I hear these sounds, I think of Mansoor, and once in a while I even feel a faint shudder on my forearm or between my thick thighs—like muscle memory, except we never touched. Sometimes—through the years—when I had conjugal relations with Gerard, or Tom, or Ben, I would close my eyes and pretend they were Mansoor.

The North Shore of Nevada is a land of sin. At first I could not understand why anyone would want to come here, despite its great beauty, situated in nature. The skiing and the hiking yes, but then these casinos with their plush carpets, the croupiers with their slicked-back hair, the illegal prostitutes waiting on street corners—some very beautiful, others as old and fat as I now am.

What would Mansoor think of me? I remember reading the Qur'an with him, his harmonic monotone as he intoned the holy scriptures. He could Khatm by heart, without looking at the Qur'an. I only completed Khatm twice, whilst looking at the Qur'an.

When they took me back to Bergen-Op-Zoom, for the first month I tried so hard to Khatm from memory, because Ibu said whoever completes a Khatm has an accepted prayer: *if Allah wishes, He gives his reward to him right in this world or He leaves it to the afterworld by bestowing him a tree in Heaven.*

But I could never remember even the first five verses of the Surah Al-Baqara.

All I remembered were inconsequential snatches I'd found beautifully strange:

And when the she-camels, ten-months pregnant, are abandoned—

Surely, man is in a state of loss—

The evil of those who blow into knots to undo them—

Sneaking whisperer into the hearts of men—

11th June 1989

I will burn in two hells.

At my funeral, however I die and whenever, I would like for little statues of the Buddha to be given out at my memorial. I have already purchased these little statues, made of bronze-plated aluminium, wrapped them in old newspapers, and packed them away at the back of my wardrobe. I wish to be cremated, lest my body be fought over in death.

On my third day as a chambermaid two years ago, I opened the bedside drawer in a resort to stow away the pay-per-view TV menu, and there I saw them, side-by-side: the Bible, the Qur'an and a laminated book with a picture of a stone Buddha on it. I was first paralysed, then I slammed the drawer shut on my finger.

I scrubbed the toilet and changed the sheets, then I reopened the drawer and took out the third book. It read *Lotus Sutra* on the front and I flipped it open:

You, the richest person in the World. Have been labouring and struggling endlessly. Not knowing that you already possess all that you seek.

After that, I sometimes opened the bedside drawers in the resorts—they don't have them in the motels—to peer at the Bible and the Qur'an lying next to one another, closed, like infants in a cot. I later found out from other Buddhist texts in the drawers that there is no singular holy book Buddhism is based upon, nor is there a creed or a one-God concept. I started reading all the Buddhist texts I found, but I would never open the Bible or the Qur'an.

Today, on a whim—though I no longer believe in Jesus or Allah—I opened the Bible with hands that trembled. This is the verse it fell upon:

Unto the woman he said, I will greatly multiply thy sorrow and thy conception; in sorrow thou shalt bring forth children; and thy desire shall be to thy husband, and he shall rule over thee.

And then I opened the Qur'an:

And thou seest the mountain which thou thinkest to be firmly fixed, but they shall pass away like the passing of the clouds—the work of Allah Who has made everything perfect. Verily, He knows full well what you do.

I peeled back the curtains and threw open the windows, looking out at the lake and the mountains, breathing in the bitingly fresh air.

Chick

YOU ONCE HELD a fluffy yellow chick in the ball of your hand when you were nine, cupping your palm around it gingerly. This was on an excursion to the zoo, and the tram had alighted at the farm animals section. It stank of goat shit and hay, and there were potbellied black pigs in a pen that you could have stared at all afternoon, disgusted by and enamoured of their sorry anatomy.

Forty of you held forty yellow chicks in hand, and you were the only one who had the urge to squeeze, you couldn't say why. You loved animals and you were a good kid. The chick's head stuck out over one end of your closed fist, and you felt its wings beat against the insides of your palm as you closed in on its small, warm body.

You only wanted to see how far you could go, like the time you ended up stapling your finger. Also the time you pushed a pearl into your left nostril. The thrilling terror in the moment, the twin flecks of blood, the momentary impediment to respiration. Except you didn't understand then the difference between doing things to yourself, and doing things to other things or people, and now, there was a dead chick in your hand.

Everyone agreed it was an accident, because you cried. You didn't start crying right away, you were answering their questions stoically. You didn't cry not because you didn't feel bad—you went home and you threw up—but because crying seemed so juvenile and hypocritical; you'd just performed a very costly experiment at the expense of a living thing. But then you saw that your impassive demeanour was arousing suspicion in the teachers questioning you, and all you had to do was cry to be let off, and so you did, because what else was there to do? What good would it be to capitulate to petty, facetious chiding when your internal landscape was burning? In that moment as your tears began to fall, blurring the small, fuzzy, yellow corpse on the table behind the zookeeper, you saw yourself perfectly.

Just one more thing on this. As they let you off, as the teachers began offering consolatory, maternal embraces and scented tissue, you saw the zookeeper drop off the chick's limp form into an organic waste bin. When everyone went for a toilet break later, you snuck back into this shed. The zookeeper wasn't in, and you reached into the bin, which was full of peat. The chick's body was still warm, and you had a dead chick in your pocket for the next four hours. You moved with a delicate fastidiousness, in the manner of someone who'd been very recently circumcised. When you got home, you buried it under a frangipani tree three doors down from your bungalow with the long driveway, in front of someone else's house. Every day, until you moved away, you placed a frangipani bloom by the stone marker you'd wedged deeply into the ground.

• • •

When you were thirteen, you were having a casual conversation with your classmate about movies, when she ended up confiding in you: she didn't understand why, when people engaged in prolonged lip-locking onscreen, she felt like urinating.

This classmate was not a close friend of yours, she just happened to be seated beside you in the class plan, which was aggregated via random assignment, in the form teacher's hopes of attenuating the classroom noise level. She was also, normatively, a nerd, whatever we make of these terms within a crude, teenaged social prism in which we hope to see ourselves favourably reflected.

And so you told her about masturbation, and what it was to be turned on, but only because *urinating* was so inelegant a misunderstanding of her immediate situation, so grossly fallacious. You were careful to preface what you were saying with the fact that you did not, yourself, masturbate (which was true) nor were you (unlike her) turned on by prolonged lip-locking onscreen. You knew these things only in theory, because you were well-read in general. You also thought it was pretty lame that mere kissing would give her a rush down south—would porn give her an aneurysm? Not that you'd seen any (true again), but *just saying*.

She listened calmly, and asked you further questions, questions that were way out of your league, which was in fact not by any measure a league at all: she and you were in an all girls' school (the best one in town, too). Everyone who gets deposited in a single sex school is placed there by parents looking to delay sexual maturation and quash emotional distraction, confident as they are of the assumedly more conducive studying environment—you knew so very little, you were not curious enough to transgress these unspoken boundaries on your own, and neither was she.

But together, by the motivating power of two, the legitimacy of having a partner in crime, you both made a unit that was collectively curious enough to want to know more. You went over to her place (Doing science project, you told your mother, which wasn't so far from the truth), and together you surfed (the verb had not yet fallen out of fashion) the internet.

By the time you went home for a late dinner, she and you had found out what scat, snuff, pegging, red rhapsody, face-sitting, *bukkake*, tentacle erotica and creampie were.

You went home, not giving it too much thought, had your dinner, did your homework, and went to bed. Subsequent days passed with no fanfare, the two of you no longer discussed masturbation et al., it was as if she'd never brought it up at all, as if you'd never gone over. Which suited you just fine, it wasn't something to be proud of, but neither were you particularly embarrassed or guilty, you'd looked upon it objectively, in the interest of satiating a faint adolescent curiosity that really wasn't a priority, though there was, you felt, some pressure to be aware of things in practice, just so you would never be the butt of any innuendo-carrying joke without knowing it, just so you were more worldly.

So it was with some surprise that you were called down to the principal's office the following week, where your sitting partner sat in-between her parents on the couch. The principal sat behind her desk. There was an empty chair before her.

Sit, the principal said by way of greeting, and you sat.

The principal explained that the parents of your sitting partner had caught her surfing snuff porn, and had then found copious amounts of porn on her computer, with the earliest saved file dating from two weeks back, the night after you went over. Your sitting partner had quickly confessed that it was you who'd led her astray, who'd told her about masturbation, suggested a virtual field trip into internet porn, and encouraged her to watch porn on a nightly basis.

When you tried to explain yourself, the principal gave you a withering look, and as you looked at your sitting partner in furious disbelief (she did not make eye contact with you, but was leaning weakly on the pudgy shoulder of her father, who was glaring savagely at you), you realised that this was because your sitting partner was at one glance, a nerd, and well, you were not a nerd. You had been booked by the prefects for having multiple ear piercings (this only meant four in your case, two on each lobe, which was nowhere near the real cool kids, who pierced their upper ear cartilage or noses or tongues or belly buttons), and your school skirt was hiked up. Your sitting partner had heavy spectacles, her skirt fell below her knees, and she still carried a cartoon-character water-bottle with a colourful woven nylon strap.

Your sitting partner's father was saying something to you, so angry that spit was gathering at either side of his mouth. The principal was dialling your home number to request the immediate presence of one or more of your parents, to alert them of their daughter's misdeeds. Her mouth formed the shape of *Hello*, and you imagined your mother on the other end of the phone. You felt her dying of shame. You wished you could protect her from this, even if not yourself.

You looked at your sitting partner's spotless school shoes and neatly rolled down socks, the Casio watch strapped tightly onto her right wrist. Your sitting partner's father was holding on to his daughter tightly even as he railed at you from his seat, and his pants were tight over his large belly and you could see the bulge of his crotch.

You gave up. You did the next best thing you could think of. You pictured him red and naked, the glandular smell of the indecently obese. You pictured your sitting partner with her father's sluggish penis in her inexperienced hands. Her hands were so small and she was so stupid, she'd wrapped two hands around it. She was so timid and inept she was massaging it side to side rather than rubbing it up and down. He was getting angry at her; spit was gathering at either side of his mouth.

• • •

For a period of time when you were in junior college, you really couldn't stop making tidy little lacerations on your forearms. To the casual viewer, things didn't add up. You were seventeen. You were popular and you were desired and you were wooed. You were on the arm of a new cute boy every week, taking names and hearts for your own. In your receipt were various items teenaged girls died trying to be given:

helium balloons, red roses, handwritten letters, typewritten poems, enormous stuffed animals, branded pencil cases, fine chocolate. Every week was Valentine's Day for you.

Yet, you were dissatisfied. You ploughed through the boys looking for something that would stop you dead in your tracks, but they were all so puerile. Till then, you would have to mark the passage of time on your arms, in the fashion of cavemen, four vertical lines, one horizontal, drawn across for quick tabulation.

Your mother cried, and then your father. They hid all the knives, and all the other tangentially sharp objects, as if they were baby-proofing the house. They conducted bag raids for blades. They brought you to a psychiatrist. Your mother offered to go in with you, and you rolled your eyes at her. As you got up to go in, you looked back at her; she looked so mortified to be alone in a shrink's waiting room.

When you went in, the back of his chair was to you. When he swivelled around, you stopped dead in your tracks.

It wasn't that he was handsome. But his ugliness was so different, so well-seasoned. Perhaps it had nothing to do with his face at all, but that his back was to you when you entered, and that he'd swivelled around. Perhaps it was simply because he was a shrink, and you were seventeen. When your parents had told you hesitantly about the appointment, anticipating your rancour, the truth was that you'd felt special.

Hello, he said, and then he held out his palms, like Jesus in the paintings.

You bared the insides of your forearms to him, allowing him to take them into his hands.

His hands didn't close in on you. He withdrew them and said: You're proud of them.

You said: That's no way to treat your patient.

He said: That's no way to treat yourself.

You sat on his chaise lounge. You told him about the emptiness. You told him about the unfledged boys who kept trying to put their hands under your skirt, how you slapped them away not because you didn't want to, but because they were insipid. If they really had you, they wouldn't know what to do with you, and you would feel embarrassed for them. You told him about the need to document and annotate time, to write on your body in your own hand. He responded gently now, asked you astute questions, nodded at all the right times, made you reveal things you never wanted to.

On your fourth appointment, when you touched him on the knee as he sat on the futon beside the chaise lounge whilst your mother waited outside, he drew away, and you were disappointed. Then you saw that his hands were trembling slightly and that's when you knew he wanted you too.

One time you said: How can you make *everyone* feel you understand them and care for them? That's not fair. I can't trust you, and he said, To be honest, I've taken a personal interest in you. Do you say that to everyone? No, I don't. You started to unbutton your school shirt, and he didn't stop you.

The day you came in on a weekend, out of your school uniform, you could see the disappointment on his face. You didn't move to sit on his glass table and remove your shirt and bra like you always did during the last ten minutes, and he didn't lick your tits and jack himself off. You'd always been afraid that he'd wanted more but he never did, only looked at your tits like they made him want to cry.

The next time you went in to see him, in your uniform, in the last five minutes, whilst he was licking your tits, you said, Doctor, how can I be paying you to lick my tits? and he must have thought you were role-playing because he licked harder and faster and you said, I'm serious, and you got off the table.

As you were putting your bra back on, he said, Please, please don't tell your parents. It'll be over for me, I worked so hard to have this clinic.

You ignored him and he said, Do you know, a body when it is seventeen, what that's like?

Of course I do.

You don't know what it's like for me. I can't even look at my wife any more.

You put on your shirt and said, Do you want to see me outside of work?

Sometimes you wished he could pick you up from school, because he drove a Porsche, but you always had to take a bus to somewhere else first.

When you got three A's for your A-Levels, he took you out for ice cream and bought you a quilted Prada bag, and that's when you asked, Do you have a daughter?

He spooned the melting honey lavender, a pale lilac, and you put your hand over his: I said, do you have a daughter?

Yes, he said finally.

How old is she?

He was twirling his spoon. You could see that he was deciding whether or not to lie.

She's three years younger than you.

You'd stopped cutting when he'd started licking your tits, and now you looked at his face and thought of saying, It's over, but instead you said, Show me a photo. When he wouldn't, you said, It's over.

• • •

A month later you were in university and you met the philosophy professor. *We are free because we lack the very language to articulate our unfreedom*, he said in a lecture theatre with four hundred students. You were seated in a non-descript locale, off to the left in the eighth row, third from the aisle, but the philosophy professor had looked right at you. He was from Poland, but he had a Russian accent. He had a beard. Only much later would you find out that he had lifted that line off of Žižek. The girl beside you was yawning. You stopped dead in your tracks.

He fucked you from behind after your very first date, and his large and hairy stomach rubbed coarsely against the smooth base of your spine. Afterwards, he fried up some bacon and you watched him in the kitchenette. You thought of how predictable you were, the way you were collecting men of specific vocations the way girls wanted ponies, the way Nabokov loved his butterflies.

You didn't tell him it was your first time. When you were both eating, he fished out your essay on the implications of Heidegger's *Being and Time* on the ethics of experience, wrote

A+ in pencil and drew a decisive circle around it, leaving a grease mark in the margin.

You started crying angrily into your bacon, thinking of how many warm young bottoms must have gone before you as you said, That's what you think of me? I'm not doing this for the grades. You got up to go but he caught you by the waist, swept away the bacon—the plates crashing to the floor—and the whole lot of essays, to take you from the front on the kitchen table. You found this gesture incredibly European. Later, you would try to explain it to him—I could never imagine an Asian man sweeping everything off the table without a care. You told him to do it to you again. Afterwards when he was cleaning up with paper napkins and you perched on the kitchen table hugging your knees to your chest, he said, *Myślę, że mógłbym cię kochać*. What's that, you said, but he wouldn't tell. He would say it ten more times before he agreed to tell you what it meant in English—I think I could love you. When the essay came back in class, you got a B for it.

A few months after you left the psychiatrist, you agreed to meet him. He'd been asking to see you every week but you'd ignored him. You met him in a café and told him you only had five minutes.

He rolled up his sleeves carefully and showed you his arms. They were way shallower than the incisions you used to make.

Try harder, you said. He began crying in the café, and you shushed him.

Finally he lifted his head and said: I'll never meet another girl like you.

I'm only special insofar as your life is boring, you said.

There was a honk from the road outside the café. It was the philosophy professor in his Audi.

The coffees you and the psychiatrist ordered had just arrived. You paid for them both and left.

• • •

Remember the chick? Forget the chick. You did this to a human being. You'd moved away from that bungalow with the long driveway and for the first time in your life you were doing your own laundry and ironing your own clothes. You were twenty-seven.

Somebody loved you and sat in the palm of your hand, and you couldn't stop squeezing. There are so many ways of making use of a person, far more than there are ways of generosity and loving. The beauty of humans, though, is that they are far less fragile than a three-week-old chick and far more adaptable. The contortions you could tease out of this human being delighted you.

We won't go into how you limned *squeezing*, nor for how long, suffice to say this human being eventually broke. There was nothing gradual nor ambiguous about it: you saw the light go out of this human being's eyes, the light specific to the torch he carried for you. Before his eyes turned cold you tried to buy him back, like Dido of Carthage pleading with Aeneas to stay as he prepared his fleet to sail away from her. *Mene fugis? ...fuit aut tibi quicquamdulce meum, miserere domus labentis, et istam*: From me are you fleeing? ... if there was anything sweet in me for you, to pity my sinking house and this.

You would even say that at this instance, for you, the spell was broken, and you were ready to love this human being back, and to atone for all the prolix squeezing. Unfortunately, the breaking of the enchantment was a two-way affair, and this human being no longer wanted anything to do with you. You'd succeeded. You'd pushed a human being to the furthest they could stand to be with you before they went off the far edge, you'd espied the precise axis at which angle you ceased to be worthy of love.

This human being looked past you even as you cradled him in your palm, as you first cooed sweet nothings and promises, and then cried. This human being broke not because he could not be stretched further, but because he saw, finally, that the squeezing was a limit you were testing in your personal vanity. It was not a test of love, as this human being had previously believed. This human being would forever be dead to you.

Laundromat

IT STARTED OUT as a 24-hour Laundromat, really, and then he saw from his little CCTV that the people in there lingered, wanting to talk to one another, wondering if they were both the same kind of lonely, but they were Asian and it was difficult. The Laundromat did not carry with it the same type of casual grungy romanticism as it did in Western countries, an invitation to treat over churning denim and cotton and underpants. Here perhaps it was something to be ashamed of—that you had no one to do your laundry for you, that you accumulated soiled clothing and found it more economical to use token-operated machines, that you were airing your dirty linen in public. So they turned away from one another, collecting their freshly laundered clothes in gaudy plastic pails and baskets, walking away from one another into the day or night.

And so the proprietor introduced the cats. Nothing fancy, just a ginger and a tortoiseshell he'd seen loitering at the nearby void deck. He was too cheap to get something pedigree, and besides he didn't think the heartland crowd might appreciate a Russian Blue or a Maine Coon much. He put red collars with shiny gold bells on them, and gave them each a bowl in the corner of the room. They did well. They were less nonchalant than he'd expected. They circled the legs of customers in infinity loops, rubbed their heads against a variety of shins, and leapt onto rumbling washing machines demanding to be stroked.

The proprietor went back to watching, and he saw the way the man was able to approach the woman because she was petting the tortoiseshell, the importance of an intermediary. He saw them sink down to the floor to tickle the tortoiseshell together when the cat stretched herself. He saw the man taking a picture of the tortoiseshell on his phone, showing it to the woman, and how they exchanged numbers afterwards.

It was a viable business. More people were coming in, and the cats acquired names. The elderly crowd—who came mainly in the day—called the tortoiseshell QQ and the ginger Ah Boy, whilst the younger ones—who came by night—called them Belle and Mittens. People coalesced around the cats, squatting to pet them. A week later, the proprietor put in an old foldable table a coffee shop had discarded, and four white stools that'd cost him only eight dollars each. He brought in his electric kettle and his mini fridge, his old study table and swivel chair. Then he went to the cheapest supermarket and bought a whole range of cup noodles and a few cartons of carbonated soda. He arranged them as a pyramid, and the ginger knocked them down after an hour. He rearranged the pyramid.

The tortoiseshell had a habit of entwining her longish tail round the proprietor's calf, but as soon as a customer walked in she would stalk over, as if the stranger owed her something. When you approach people with clarity, it is perhaps difficult for them to not reciprocate. More often than not, they would put down their laundry and tickle her under the chin. The proprietor had never thought of keeping a pet because he thought he'd make a bad owner, but he saw then that not all living things pin all their hopes and dreams on you. Life goes on and it was egotistical to imagine otherwise.

In the last week of the first month of the Laundromat's opening, he brought in the second-hand bracket-mounted television set and the karaoke system with the amps. He'd personally selected all the songs loaded up in the CDs—mournful, melodramatic songs of heartbreak and loss across Chinese, Cantonese and English. Steve Chou's 'Dusk', Shirley Kwan's dream pop take on Teresa Teng's 'Forget Him', even Johnny Cash's 'Folsom Prison Blues'.

The first hesitant middle-aged woman who approached him wanted to know if she had to pay to use the karaoke system.

No, as long as you're a customer here.

She indicated her wash and he nodded to her and asked if he could help to rig her song up. He offered her the song list with two hands. He'd typed out the available songs and laminated the printout at the stationery shop next door. There were air bubbles at the edges. She chose Sandy Lam's 'In Love With Someone Who Never Comes Home'.

In love with someone who never comes home
Awaiting the opening of a stolid front door
Inconstant gaze, tightly sealed lips
Why pursue bitterness?

When the song ended, she had tears in her eyes. She asked, Is there a limit to the number of songs I can sing?

No.

She sang till the sun set. QQ and Ah Boy, morphing into Belle and Mittens, were asking to be fed. Her clothes had completed their spin dry hours ago and he'd helped her to remove them into her kingfisher blue plastic pail. A small audience had gathered and dispersed across the three hours she'd sung. Customers of the Laundromat watching her with a canned drink in hand, schoolchildren on their way home passing by en route to the McDonald's at the neighbourhood town centre, the uncles who hung out outside the barbershop two doors down, mothers with NTUC supermarket plastic bags laden with groceries.

When she finally put down the microphone, there was a smattering of applause. She looked a little flustered, as if she weren't sure how she'd ended up here. She turned to the proprietor and said, Thank you. She left forgetting her fresh laundry, and the proprietor ran after her, pail in hand. When he got back, an old man had taken to the microphone. He'd dialled up Liu Fong's "You Made Me Happy Once". Before he began singing, he said to the proprietor, Know what you need to sing well?

What?

Dead knots in your heart.

The proprietor's hours in the Laundromat were not fixed, but he tended towards the hours between noon and midnight. When he wasn't in the Laundromat, he would place a metal till with a slot for money for the self-service canned drinks and cup noodles, with a felt-tip pen sign on the counter to pay a dollar for a drink and a dollar fifty for the noodles in the four official languages. He woke often in the middle of the night and when he did, he enjoyed watching the CCTV. Even when there was no one there, he could watch Belle curled up on the table or Mittens swatting a lizard. Sometimes when both cats weren't in, he would feel afraid that he would never see them again, but they always returned.

Twice, in the dead of the night on separate occasions, he saw an old lady and a teenager help themselves to noodles or a drink without making payment. The old lady was a Laundromat customer and she helped herself to the electric kettle and slurped up her noodles seated on the plastic stool. After she was done, she took a long time selecting her brand and flavour of drink, finally deciding on ice cream soda, which somehow surprised him. The teenager ran in, swiped the noodles, and ran out. There was a middle-aged man who came in with a much younger woman one Friday night, and they'd tried to sing a duet on Jacky Cheung's 'Cuts Like A Knife'. There was only one microphone, but the woman held an invisible one in her right fist, manoeuvring it to accommodate movements of her head. There were the foreign workers on a Sunday night who made up their own Tamil lyrics to keep beat with the sprawling Cantonese instrumentals. They finished up his entire supply of cup noodles, and left money for the whole lot, with a small tip.

One night he woke to the CCTV showing a girl alone in the Laundromat. She sat atop a machine, Belle was in her lap and she was singing Simon & Garfunkel's 'The Sound of Silence'. He watched her from his laptop and thought, I've waited all my life for someone to sing 'The Sound of Silence' in a Laundromat. He could have brushed his teeth and put on a clean shirt and taken a cab over and he would probably have been able to catch her, but he didn't. It was difficult for him to relate to people without abstraction.

He went into the Laundromat early the next day, at six in the morning, petted QQ and Ah Boy, and opened the mouth of the machine she'd used. He merely wanted to smell the washing powder she used, but he saw something dark in the reel. He fished out a pair of red nylon panties. He held it apart, filling in the detail of her hips and thighs in the negative space. He folded it delicately in his handkerchief and kept it in his pocket.

When he got home later that evening, he would resist the urge to place it into a Ziploc, to tag it. He hated the way he always needed to label things and people; he wished he could simply observe—and partake—but for him order and classification had always been paramount, even as a child. The more he looked at the red panties, the less and less it looked like underwear.

The proprietor was in fact an urban anthropologist. He could only look at things at arm's length. If he wanted to get closer, he could only do so if he was studying it. The Laundromat was a social experiment-cum-community-study that had received a grant from a university department interested in profiling social loneliness in urban density and the potential of interaction and ownership that could be initiated by ground-level tenancy in low-income housing estates. The Laundromat would be open for only six months in this old estate bordering Chinatown, and there would be student assistants who would work shifts sitting at the stools incognito, taking field notes from the second month onwards, when the situation was thought to have stabilised and behavioural patterns would have been set in motion.

For months after the closure of the Laundromat, the student assistants will replay the footage ad nauseum on the old monitors in the university's Attitudes & Social Cognition Lab, one booth each with headphones on. The urban anthropologist will begin referring to the student assistants by the month they are in charge of. Can I see that transcript, November? Hey, August: do you think you could do up stats for the correlation between chair type and the length of time people spent in the Laundromat?

One day, as October serves up his morning coffee, she'll ask, Professor, don't we need longitudinal studies? Don't you want to know if the residents miss the place? If there was a reversion of behaviour? He'll bite the end of a pen and say: That's not within the scope of this study, October. October will press on, But Professor, isn't it unethical to give people something they want and need, knowing you will soon take it away from them? The urban anthropologist will remember the section of the grant paperwork he'd pussyfooted with academic jargon, under the header *Impact on Community*. Remembering this will irritate him. October, the urban anthropologist will say, tapping his foot steadily, we are sociologists, not politicians. We are academics, not charity workers. Life is a phenomenon.

QQ was rubbing her head on his shin. He touched her under her chin and she purred. He wanted to ask QQ what the girl smelled like, and if her skin was soft.

The red nylon panties in the urban anthropologist's pocket felt like a paperweight. He felt like it was difficult to go on now, but he was also old enough to know that life doesn't change because you feel something at a certain point in time. If he wanted to, he could pay a sex worker to put on the red panties later tonight and he could push the fabric at the crotch to the side and fuck her with the panties on. He preferred experiencing things second-hand, with a delay, a justification or a proxy to soften the blow of *life*.

At nine in the morning, two wheezing old men dropped a rattan sofa in front of the Laundromat.

Are you the boss, one of them asked in Mandarin.

I suppose you could say so, the urban anthropologist said.

This is the best thing that's happened to this neighbourhood.

Thank you.

We like this place, and we want to hear people sing while we wait for our clothes to tumble dry, but there aren't enough seats. One of us saw this whilst passing the dump and we thought we'd bring it over to see what you think. What do you think?

The urban anthropologist looked from the two old men to the worn sofa and back to the men again. I think it's great, he said.

There, one old man said to the other, mopping his brow, I told you it wouldn't be a waste of our labour.

We walked three blocks, the other old man said. It was a gamble.

The urban anthropologist turned to the fridge, took out

two cans of Kickapoo and opened them for the old men. They lounged on the rattan sofa with QQ and Ah Boy, and he joined them. One of the men was stroking the length of QQ, looking through the song list and chastising the urban anthropologist for not having the Hokkien song 'If I Had A Million Bucks', or the Teresa Teng favourite 'The Moon Represents My Heart'.

Why are they all sad songs?

Happy songs are jarring, so you have to keep updating. I don't have time for that. Sad songs are more timeless.

Don't you want the people who come here to be happy?

Being able to be sad is a form of happiness too.

The old man stared at the urban anthropologist as if he were waiting for him to say he was only pulling his leg. The urban anthropologist was silent. The old man brought the lip of the can to his mouth, taking a deep swig. He said: Well, young man, then, what you need here is beer.

How's business, the other old man wanted to know. Will you survive? He looked at the floor and mumbled, My old woman is gone. I don't want to go back to hand washing my clothes again.

We're okay for now, the urban anthropologist said, but who is to say what the future holds?

True, true, the old man said as he clasped his hands behind his back, the only certainty in life is uncertainty.

The introductory bars of Anita Mui's 'Looks Like An Old Friend's Returned' were playing across the system. Ah Boy leapt off the sofa, followed by QQ. The other old man pressed pause. The TV froze on a still of a cascading waterfall, with the lyrics appearing on the bottom of the screen, the first Chinese character beginning to light up in pink. The old man who'd pressed pause was looking at a stain on the sofa. He suggested they wash the faded floral coverlets. They stripped the cushions bare and the urban anthropologist loaded up the machine.

Siren

The Merlion is a mythical creature with the head of a lion and the body of a fish, used as a mascot and national personification of Singapore. The fish body represents Singapore's origin as a fishing village when it was called Temasek, or 'sea town' in Javanese. The lion head represents Singapore's original name—Singapura—meaning 'lion city' or 'kota singa'.

The symbol was designed in 1964 by Alec Fraser-Brunner, a member of the Souvenir Committee and curator of the Van Kleef Aquarium, for the logo of the Singapore Tourism Board (STB). Although STB replaced the Merlion as its corporate logo in 1997, the board continues to regulate the use of the Merlion symbol. With the exception of souvenirs conforming to specific guidelines, members of the public are not allowed to produce artefacts featuring the Merlion or anything that resembles it without seeking permission from the board. According to the STB Act, failure to comply with these regulations could result in a $1,000 fine per artefact.

HE TARGETS THE tourists, sarong party boy. They want something local and exotic, as all tourists do, and what could be more *experiential*, really, than a romp with him. Orchard Towers is where he plies his trade, vying for the indiscreet staring and propositioning with the Eastern European pretties in the leather minis and the docile Southeast Asians with their nasal sing-song voices. The finger-pointing and bad-mouthing fall in the wake of his path like so much confetti. He's learned to revel in it, gracious as a beauty queen.

Here we're brought up to call a spade a freak with such backhand ease. His name is Marl, and he sat at the back of class trying for the cool pallor of indifference, but his little-boy heart was breaking.

Your father is a lion! Your mother is a fish! we used to chant riotously behind him, before him, beside him.

Already he'd looked so different—his pale skin a sick shade of grey, always covered with a light film of sweat, large eyes, jagged milk teeth strangely juxtaposed with lips too full for a boy, lips he pulled at like a catapult when he was nervous—but we'd laid off him because he was quiet. We ribbed him discreetly amongst ourselves but we never laid a finger on him, until he blurted out once: My mother is a mermaid.

And then we were light-headed with relief because now he'd done it, given us a reason. Which self-respecting boy would say something like that? He deserved our ridicule, and we gave it to him in full force. We laughed boorishly. We drew pictures of his mother with breasts, seashells on her nipples. We drew pictures of what we imagined copulation between a boy and a mermaid would look like. We were graphic when it came to imagining where they would stick it in.

At some point, one of these drawings surfaced to a teacher. Marl wasn't the one who'd turned it in, we knew this, for between all boys—even the bullying and the bullied—there is a code of honour that is seldom transgressed.

We were called in for questioning. She gave each of us three light raps across the knuckles, with a wooden ruler. Marl's only making things up because he lost his mother, the teacher said, we should be ashamed of ourselves. None of us were. We were itching to get at him—someone had to take the discontent of our being ratted on, what more convenient a scapegoat than a victim?

The good intentions of the teacher were completely flushed away by the time we were done with his head and the toilet bowl. At the end of it, we called him a liar, an orphan.

To which he said, No, I have a father.

Sure we remembered—we'd seen his father once, waiting for him by the school gate. He looked like a rangy beast, with a head of coarse and curly long hair, and a face obscured by whiskers and stubble. Lionhead, said one of us in a hoarse whisper as we crept past the school gate, and it stuck.

Your father is a lion! Your mother is a fish!

Lionhead fucked a mermaid, out comes a freak.

My father is a sailor, Marl said. I live on a house made of sticks that floats on the sea. His hair was dripping toilet water. We laughed at his hollow boast.

Liar liar pants on fire,

Suck your pacifier.

He snivelled wearily, drawing the back of a hand across his nose. We were quite prepared to let him off right then, until one of us thought to bring up a little rumour that'd circulated that very morning, right before the teacher had called us in—a boy in our class had been at the urinals at the same time as Marl, and came back reporting that what was between Marl's legs didn't seem to be what the rest of us boys had.

So what did it look like?

Different.

What did it look like!

I don't know.

Was it just tiny? Deformed?

I *don't* know!

The truth is, we were generally in silent agreement that our classmate was lying, given his unwillingness to substantiate, and our class's propensity to tease Marl. Except that when we relayed this episode, Marl's eyes flew open wildly, and he punched one of us. Never before had he retaliated. Now we closed in on him uproariously, four boys packed into a toilet cubicle, three standing, one crouching.

Two of us pinned him down, leaving me to move in on Marl. Marl was kicking and screaming but we held fast. I took his bermudas off and we were laughing forcefully, pronouncedly, laughter as a swagger. Marl was sobbing, snot entering his mouth.

I hesitated, and the other two of us repeated in quick succession, like a cheer, like a warning: *Your father is a lion! Your mother is a fish!* I knew the code of honour, I knew they were leaving it to me to be pack leader, cavalier and cruel. I moved towards him again, with exaggerated motions.

Marl looked into my face, our eyes met, and I saw that there was terror in his. He closed his eyes and said through gritted teeth, *Please, no.*

I stopped and picked up his bermudas in a sudden awkward movement.

Let's see who can string this from the classroom fan, I boomed, and arranged my posture to suggest sprinting out of the toilet. If they bought it, we would run out in three, two, *one.*

They released Marl. We ran out. I held Marl's bermudas above my head like a flag, and it became a race to reach the classroom first. When we reached the classroom, I volleyed the bermudas to them like a ball, and they received it like dogs, aiming it to land smack on the ceiling fan blade. They kept missing.

I went back to the toilet. Marl was still curled up in a corner of the cubicle, in his school shirt and underwear. I held out a hand to help him to his feet. He took it, and when I pulled him up, he dragged on the momentum and hemmed me into a hug. In his arms I could feel his gratitude, and his pale skin was soft. But everyone knows you can never embrace another boy, everyone knows what it means, and he was in his underwear for god sakes. I shouted, *Pansy, wuss, faggot!* Then I punched him for good measure and walked briskly out of the toilet.

Marl didn't come back to class.

In the middle of the week, Lionhead came to collect Marl's school bag, his wallet and his textbooks. At the end of the week, our form teacher cancelled his name on the register whilst taking attendance.

We found new targets, but we went easier on them. We pegged his name as an insult—*Dude, you are as fucked up as Marl.* Primary school ended and we went on to secondary school, single sex and all boys as well, where bullying was no longer such a blood sport—we rarely went all out, as long as the freaks knew their place—and we began noticing girls. An overhead bridge away from us was an all-girls secondary school, with neat white skirts to their knees.

Every so often, through the years, I dreamt of him. Always in the white school shirt, the white underwear; sometimes in his arms. Always the flaming curiosity of what was in between his legs. Sometimes, reaching out to try to satiate that curiosity with my hands. That was always the point at which I woke, a safety valve as it were. I would always wake before I touched, before I saw, in a furtive sweat. Then the shame of going to the toilet, feeling the viscous wet, washing and wringing my underwear.

• • •

There was once a hirsute man who was a sailor for a British shipping company. When that dried up, he got by as a fisherman. Anything so long as he could be near water. And do you believe in sirens? Not of the Greek mythology stock—the Southeast Asian variety featured ashen complexions set off by kelp-like hair, deadened eyes and garoupa-scaled tails.

Why the hirsute sailor and the ashen siren hooked up is completely up for speculation: if you'd been lost at sea for two days and two nights in a storm and a disembodied singing voice lures you into crashing your sampan—that is, your livelihood—onto craggy rocks, one would think you would be looking to wreak vengeance on the source of the voice, not fall into her arms—gnarly and cold—and copulate—for which she had to split her tail to welcome your appendage.

The capsized fisherman had stalked out of the water like a bull, emerging from his smashed ship like a singular seed from a pod. She lay askew on the shore, tail twitching slightly. Her eyes shone in the dark like a cat's. She issued her siren song, a reedy, strangled moan in varying pitches.

Sire me a son, she whispered in pidgin Malay, slowing down his fury. The waves crashed as the wind howled and he scarcely saw the movement of her lips, but the words were unmistakeable, like a spell. As she said this, as he slowed, she parted her tail with her hands, as if slowly splitting an elongated husk to reveal virginal white flesh within. My world is your oyster, she sang softly, All it needs is one grain of sand.

His hands trembled as he lowered his drab olive fisherman pants, lay down on this cold dirty beach, and slid into her as the waves ebbed and flowed. She was cold and slippery to the touch; as he climaxed, he almost rode right off of her. He'd placed his face close to hers, and she smelled of sea spray in a more fundamental way than sea spray itself.

When he was done, as he was stumbling off the sand and dusting the sharp, gravelly bits from his knees, it occurred to him that her back might have hurt from the same. He wiped his palms against one another, cradled her into a sitting position—she was strangely pliant—and cleaned the bits of sand pressed into her pale back.

It was this gesture that saved his life. She'd already thought about breaking his neck between her tail muscles, leaving the body out to bake and decompose on the shore, the quotidian sharing of meat with others of her ilk alongside crabs and gulls, as they did with her.

She relinquished her grasp on the two ends of her tails, and they began to seal seamlessly beneath the ligaments and scales. Watching this retreat, he was seized by a fervid inspiration, and gently but firmly pried her tail ends back, as if parting the legs of a docile woman supine in the village fields.

She found herself allowing him this transgression. When he'd parted her far back enough and what he sought was back in view, he leaned down and buried his face in her cleft.

It was only then she writhed and thrashed. What went before had been for her but a grim inveiglement; this, this was something new and unexpected.

She tasted of oysters, raw but for a sprinkling of salt.

They spent the night spooning in the recess of a huge, half-rotted log, softened by the moisture of the sea, ingrown with algae. When they came apart, her back was lukewarm, heated by his hirsute chest.

Before daylight broke, she showed him how to fashion a raft from halved banana tree trunks that they hacked at with jagged stones. To hold them together, she gave him her hair, black as squid ink and hardy as twine.

Together they pushed the raft out to sea. On the sand, she moved like a cripple, upper body weight supported by her tail and both hands. In water, she was indistinguishable from the easy grace of the waves. As they headed further out into the sea, he realised with each step that he could imagine a life with her. It wouldn't amount to much, and he might never see his family and friends again, but that didn't seem important. They could explore the reefs, lay thrown out on rocks like shipwrecks, spear fish for meals, couple on the sand. He'd dive for saltwater pearls for her. Braid them into her hair as she slept.

A hand on the raft, he turned back with the intent of asking her if he really had to leave. She spoke before he did.

Say nothing—you must go.

I will return to see you.

You will not—our island is on no map, found only through our song. I will never sing to you again. You must never return.

But—a son—you said you wanted a son.

This is what we say to every sailor, for that is our song. We are the black widows of the sea. We can never have a child by a mortal. The womb does not fruit.

You have my heart. How will I live?

If you stay, I will break your neck between my tail tonight. If I don't, they will find you, and you will wish you were never born. The last sailor, they ate alive. I recall the jelly of his sclera.

• • •

Hey stranger, the transsexual says.

He's beautiful, really, with his large eyes and full lips, features far sharper than all the girls in the room, very pale, and though I'm on my fifth shot and quite wasted, I'm not that adventurous. I have my eye on a Vietnamese plain Jane in a silver dress in the corner, the one with large, soft-looking breasts spilling over just so.

I'm sorry, I don't swing that way. I say it politely, with a tip of my shot glass.

It's Marl, remember? You used to stick your foot out to trip me, just like everyone else.

He flutters his false eyelashes, mimics: *Your father is a lion! Your mother is a fish!*

My breath catches in my chest and a blind panic rises in my diaphragm. It makes me want to bolt, or to hit this beautiful thing in front of me. He is watching me, and smiling. It makes his mouth feminine, a mouth done up neatly in matte red lipstick.

I run a hand through my hair and try to still myself. Just a quick, awkward hello-goodbye and it'll be over.

God, Marl. What are you doing here?

Marl takes the question in his stride. His smile grows broader.

I could ask you the same.

It's been—how long?

Fourteen years. We were twelve, weren't we? He touches his left cheek subtly, and I remember punching him.

I'm sorry.

That's all right. Boys will be boys, won't they?

You transferred schools after that. I always felt guilty for that.

No honey, I stopped going to school after that.

I am silent. I down my shot and it tastes of culpability. The Vietnamese plain-Jane is headed in this direction, perhaps she's seen me staring at her chest. Marl sees her too, sees my contemplation, and closes in on me like a big cat, all lethal grace.

Don't you want to know, after all these years? I'll give you a good price.

What?

I sputter a little. He says it with such confidence, as if he's been privy to my dreams over the years, watching unseen from the wings. He is so close I can smell the sweet perfume from the curve where his neck meets his shoulders.

You owe it to me. It's been a slow week. Think of it as a favour you won't regret.

If you really need it, I could just give you the money, Marl.

He's splashed his margarita in my face, on my chest. The bartender has signalled for the bouncer to come over. I see the bouncer making a beeline for Marl, from behind him. I see Marl tense up. I see the other people in the pub turning our way, the expression on their faces alternating as they look from Marl to me—as they take in the details: the transsexual in the tight dress, the man in the soaked shirt—derision for him, commiseration for me.

The bouncer is an elbow away, and the prurient pub crowd will have their collective gratification of seeing Marl led out by the arm in a moment. *Freak*, someone says, loudly enough to cut across the buzz of the room.

Just before the bouncer taps Marl on the shoulder, I pull him to me. His waist is at once taut and slender. The bouncer's raised hand falters.

Everything is okay here, I say.

• • •

Every so often the hirsute sailor went out in his boat, circling the waters of the strait, but never again could he find that islet, through calm seas or stormy waters. He left his kampung to live on a kelong to feel closer to her. Sometimes it seemed clear he must never have met her; she was the ignis fatuus of a delirious sailor who had found land in a sea storm. Perhaps he'd made a hole in the sand to receive his desire. Perhaps he'd fashioned the raft on his own accord, held together by dark twine that resembled the hair of a siren, not vice versa.

Then the morning he awoke with her song in his head, months later. He fought wakefulness for as long as he could, afraid as he was that it would draw away her song. He was a refugee in anything that peddled her, clutching desperately at half-formed straws. But when he finally pulled himself off the bed—a thin mattress on the rough wooden flooring—the song was still pellucid. Then he knew it wasn't just a dream.

He got into his boat, and found himself on a prepense trajectory, quite out of his hands. A small strip of land, an island that was populated with a smattering of people—he'd been here before, the people were twenty years behind the urbanites of the hinterland, he'd felt far more comfortable here. As he got out of his boat, the song did not end. He moved as he saw fit, through dirt paths, undergrowth. At every turn he ached for her to come into view. He was beside himself with discomposure, his hands shaking, the sound of a snapping twig deafening. Half an hour later he was moving towards a small, decrepit beach to the north of the island. As he stepped onto the sand, the song stopped abruptly.

He scanned the small shore in a frenzy—she was not there. There were weeping figs near the sand, and as he approached them, he saw the bundle amongst the thick roots, composed of woven leaves and lined in a mulch of seaweed. The infant that slept within; the fruition that she'd said was impossible.

He began crying in anguish. What he wanted wasn't a child, but the siren. He would have been a loving father, if the mother of the child were in the equation. The child looked normal enough, but what would he do with this aberration of nature? He knew nothing of caring for a small living thing.

He wanted to leave the child there, on the remote shore, in the roots. He wanted to destroy the child with his bare hands—he'd spent only one night with the siren, and this child had spent nine months with her, inside her. The thought was more than he could bear.

Yet the closest he could ever get to her was this. He picked the bundle up, and the child did not stir.

• • •

Marl's put on classical music. It was too quiet before, after I'd placed the five hundred dollars on the bedside table. Tuning the hotel room hi-fi, passing Techno beats, Mandarin ballads, the Top 40, sentimental oldies, interspersed with static.

The string orchestra straining, now we're talking.

What he has between his legs, is a tail. At least four inches in length, silver grey, the finned tips of the tail with a touch of yellow.

And that was Mozart's Sinfonia Concertante, *as performed by the Academy of St. Martin in the Fields.*

We do nothing for a long while, just sit on the bed with his legs spread, my head between his knees like a midwife.

And next up, a soubrette from the opera Tartuffe, *performed by the Bellevue Philharmonic for your pleasure.*

It is moist yet scaly, soft yet sharp, depending on the angle. It is retractable, nothing but a cleft visible from the outside when he pulls it in. It reappears slowly, moistened and glistening. It wiggles urgently when I try to touch it, like a fish out of water. My hand jerks back too as a reflex, but his tail's spurt of movement, the attempt to escape my touch, has rippled thrill through my body.

I try again, more forcefully this time, and the tail doesn't shrink away. I stroke it, and Marl begins moaning, very softly. I wrap my palm around it and quicken the motions of my hand, and soon Marl is clenching the sheets.

After I've taken him from behind, Marl reclines onto the headboard, sighing. His tone has lost the octave of pleasure, it is an exhalation of the unhinging of certain weight carried over from an older place, as if this is vindication, in my face, which then again, of course it is.

Missa Papae Marcelli, *a piece of compositional virtuosity from Giovanni Pierluigi da Palestrina, this rendition under the baton of Riccardo Muti.*

Marl smiles at me as if he's won, but the smile is gracious and kind. It's the smile of a winner, but it wraps around me like a coat of understanding, inclusive and indulgent. It's the kind of smile all men want to receive from all the females—mothers, wives, mistresses, sisters—in their lives, lines blurred, rolled up together.

He dozes lightly into the thick pillow, the shadow of the smile still on the fullness of his lower lip. His hair falls loosely over his shoulders and fans across the pillow. The duvet is thrown across his slim torso, leaving his crotch uncovered.

The tail is no longer to be seen, and all that there is is the sweet little cleft.

It is the cleft that reassures me. Watching him sleep thus, it is easy enough to believe that I'd just made love to a woman, that my enjoyment was not untoward. I carry this thought into sleep.

• • •

There was a storm and the kelong was rocking, the way a long carpet might when pulled from under a person. Yet the hirsute sailor and the beautiful boy of about sixteen were still out on the flimsy pier made of ferrules of cheap wood bound together and driven like stakes into the seabed.

If you were near enough, if the waves and thunder weren't crashing, you would hear the boy singing in a thin yet exquisite voice. You would see that the man had in his hands the ends of a large fishing net, and that fish were swimming into it blindly, as if drawn by invisible bait.

The hirsute sailor nodded at the boy and he stopped singing. He swung the net around and began hauling the catch out of the sea. They would keep enough for their meals and sell the rest to the fishmongers when they came later. The fishmongers always marvelled at the volume and scope of their catch. Tilapia, peacock bass, trevally, snapper and even daggertooth pike.

The hirsute sailor and the boy had a boat, but they rarely set foot on the main island, only once a month for dried groceries, and even then they often got the fishmongers to purchase their groceries for them in exchange for a catty of fish.

Life was simple. When they weren't fishing, they spent their time seated by the pier, darning their nets, looking out at the water. The boy had long, dark hair that hung to his waist, and ever since he stopped going to school, the hirsute sailor never made him shear it. Sometimes, he braided little trinkets into the boy's hair.

• • •

I open my eyes and Marl is lying on his side, back in his sequined, low-cut dress, watching me. He lays a hand on my hip. He has drawn the curtains and it is dark outside, but faintly distended with impending dawn.

Marl says: Take me somewhere?

Following his directions, we reach a jetty. I've never been this far out, surely this must be the southernmost tip of the island. Marl takes two fifty-dollar bills from the ten I've given him, tucked into his purse. I wait for him in the car. The grey sheen of his skin is apparent by the coming daylight, losing the pale iridescence it maintained by night, subtly refracting artificial white light.

A man is waiting at the end of the jetty, silhouetted fuzzily against the sea at dawn, at his feet a small cooler. Marl opens it and peers in, then hands over the money. He comes back with the cooler in hand and says, One more place?

We end up outside a compound painted a sickly green, with a sign that reads: Brightcare Old Folks' Home for the Mentally Infirm. Marl unlatches the gate and lets us both in, the cooler in his other hand.

Nurses nod grimly at him, taking in the skin-tight dress, the high heels, the heavy make-up. An old man on a wheelchair hoots at him merrily, and Marl gives him a big wink. There is the smell of piss, and pine-flavoured floor cleaner.

Marl makes a left, and we enter a room of six elderly persons. One woman sits rigidly upright, drool oozing down her chin, muttering, three other men are asleep, one snoring loudly. One man has playing cards laid out on his bed, arranged in a cryptic manner. He is cautious of my gaze as he flips the cards open. The last bed holds an old man who is tied down by both wrists. He is painfully thin.

Papa, I'm here, Marl says. I brought you your favourite.

He makes a lunge for Marl, but because both his wrists are bound, it is an awkward motion, and it is his bird-thin chest that bobs forward abruptly. He still has a shock of matted white hair, Lionhead.

Marl takes out black leather gloves from his handbag, and puts them on smoothly. For a moment I imagine him strangling this emaciated man in his bed. Then he slides back the lid of the cooler.

In it, oysters, at least two dozen. Marl picks out a shucking knife from his handbag, sits in a dark blue plastic chair, crosses his legs. He unhinges the valves of the oyster, twisting the knife around till it makes a little pop. It is an optimistic, celebratory sound, like corkage, the sound heralding the death of an oyster.

His father is salivating, like Pavlov's dogs. Also, he has a hard-on—you can see it through the thin, pale green nursing home pants. Marl brings the first oyster towards his father's waiting, gaping mouth, and the old man laps at it. Marl cups his gloved hand under the shell so his father won't cut his lower lip on the ridges.

It's the only thing he'll eat, Marl says softly, the softest he has spoken all this while. The only thing that makes him happy.

After a while, the old man begins to croon. Absurd, happy sounds, a lack of self-consciousness most complete. The muttering and snoring fall into a strange soundscape, unified by his croons. The man in the bed next to him opens up the last card, the Jack of Spades, and declares emotionlessly, with certainty, *I've lost an ocean.*

As if that is his cue, Marl stands up in his three-inch heels and stacks up the empty oyster shells that are on the veneered bedside table. He fiddles around inside the cooler and takes out one last oyster. He dislodges it and extends the oyster before my face. I pause, then bend forward to eat out of his hand. As my teeth graze the shell lightly, I remember that it is a living, breathing organism on my tongue. The oyster tastes just like him, and I swallow.

The Ballad of Arlene & Nelly

Why didn't Arlene go to the doctor when the lump first appeared?

It wasn't always this good, and Arlene never lets herself forget that. This is why she hasn't gone to the doctor's yet, despite the burgeoning lump in between the end of her armpit and the beginning of her breast, on her left side. Arlene was deeply fatalistic. Leftwards, for her, was a jinx, where unpropitious things happened.

Nelly is back, Arlene hears her key through the door, imagines her slipping off her leather shoes, and those low, thin nude socks. It never ceases to amaze Arlene when Nelly comes home.

What is the history of Arlene & Nelly?

Three periods, over the course of thirty years.

The first:

When Arlene was ten, she fell into a canal outside the school gate. Nelly was right behind her. It is still strange to them both, how she fell in. Arlene would describe being lifted off her feet, then scrabbling across the gravel and mud only to find herself in the canal, the left of her frame scraping the sharpness of its maw. Nelly said it looked like she decided to jump in. Arlene would roll her eyes at this. Arlene remembers Nelly's skirt billowing overhead as she scaled the sides of the canal to help her out, her white cotton underwear, Nelly's fringe plastered to her forehead as she stretched out an arm, the afternoon sun behind her.

The scabs along Arlene's left arm and calf were epic. Nelly walked up to her one recess-time: *Can I peel them?* The bell rang. Yes, Arlene said. For a while it was a game, and Nelly fussed over Arlene with tissue she wetted on her tongue every time she drew blood. She collected Arlene's scabs in the groove of her classroom desk, where the other girls stowed their pencils. The other girls in class, noticing this, wanted to try too. No, Nelly said to them as she rolled Arlene's sleeve up, she's mine.

After Arlene's wounds healed, their friendship grew boring. They drifted apart quickly, Nelly moving on to the company of the only girl in class who had a pager. Arlene's scars took a decade to fade.

The second:

When Arlene met Nelly again, they were nineteen, at the state teachers' college, a month before term commenced. Arlene stared and stared across the crowded room awaiting the pre-admission medical check-up, but Nelly never looked once in her direction.

Arlene had always been quiet by nature, but after they'd peed into tiny cups, pressed their breasts to X-ray machines and changed out of the medical-blue shifts, she went up to Nelly. She did not say hi; merely stood in Nelly's way. They remained this way for almost a full minute, until Arlene rolled up the sleeve on her left arm. When Nelly saw the long scar, she started laughing a husky laugh, leaning forward to embrace Arlene in recognition. Arlene placed her arms carefully around Nelly. Nelly's hair was damp and her shampoo smelled of lavender.

They shared a room at the National Institute of Education. By the end of their second year, it came to be known that they were more than friends. They'd never been seen displaying public affection, but a friend of a friend in their class had walked in on two spooning bodies one morning when she'd meant to return Arlene her tennis racquet. Their dorm-issue single beds were pushed together in the middle of the room, covered by a queen-sized duvet. The friend had slipped out quietly without waking the pair, returning the tennis racquet later in the afternoon after knocking on the door, but the revelation made its rounds.

There was the occasional lesbian couple in every cohort in every college, but there were always easy surface clues—a butch-femme dynamic, the laissez faire of holding hands in public, superficial proclivities towards piercings or closely cropped hair. The pairing off of Nelly and Arlene, however, was a great surprise to most of their cohort-mates, because they both came across as inordinately conservative.

The truth of the matter was that although Nelly and Arlene were in love as they knew it, there was also the understanding that this arrangement would hold only as long as they were in college together. Rather, this was what Nelly had always insinuated, and what kept Arlene up at night.

As they went from freshmen to sophomores, there was an anxiety about Arlene that became increasingly pronounced.

She never forgot that, each day, she was incrementally closer to losing Nelly. In her senior year, she found herself snapping at friends, crying whilst watching TV commercials.

The third:

When Arlene received the invitation card, she burnt it on her stove. Then she pressed her left palm cleanly onto the stove, the ashes swirling around. The blister was so large that a plaster couldn't cover the diameter of it and she had to bandage her hand. It'd been five years, they were twenty-seven. She imagined Nelly deciding between lilies and peonies.

At the dinner reception, Arlene was seated to the back of the ballroom. All she saw of Nelly was a head of coiffed hair seated upfront, bare shoulders glowing in an ivory gown. Throughout the dinner, there was a video projection of congenial photos of the bride and groom with their old friends. There were no pictures of Arlene and Nelly together. Her old acquaintances at the table tried to make conversation with her, but Arlene was silent. Course by course, the banquet servers cleared plate after untouched plate of food placed before Arlene.

Towards the end of the dinner, the emcee hustled everyone to their feet. Now everyone, it's time for my favourite part—*yam seng*. Remember, the longer you hold the note *yam*, the more happiness to the bride and groom. The emcee took a theatrically deep breath.

Arlene didn't even inhale, but she couldn't stop holding the note.

Yaaaaaaaaaaaaaaaaaaaaaaaaaaaaaaaaaaaaaaaaaaaaaaaaaaaaa aaaaaaaaaaaaaaaaaaaaaaaammmmmmmmmmmmmmmmmmmmmmm mmmmmmmmmmmmmmmmmmmmmmmmmmmmmmmmm mmmmmmmmmmmmmmmmmmmmmmmmmmmm

—she'd gone on longer than everyone at her table, everyone in the ballroom, and the emcee, who'd gone a little blue in the face from trying to match her, was spluttering slightly.

Everyone'd turned to her, she sounded like she was screaming in anguish; finally there was no more breath left in her, and she stopped short, feeling as if her throat and heart were on fire. She turned squarely to look at Nelly, and for the first time that night Nelly looked directly at her, her face inscrutable under all that make-up. The emcee had finally caught his breath, he lifted a hand as if conducting an orchestra, trying to rouse the guests back to complete the toast—

Seng!

Arlene excused herself from the dinner table, where a peach cream cake was being served. She found her way to the bathroom and locked herself into a stall.

There was a rap on the door. She opened it. Nelly entered the cubicle, cumbersome in the volume of her gown, and latched the door.

Why did you even invite me?

How could I not?

Why did you even invite me!

I hoped you would be happy for me.

What about my happiness?

It is yours to pursue.

Do you love him?

Stop talking like you're in a movie.

Do you love him!

Yes!

Nelly, I'll let you walk away now. But if I ever see you again—I'll kill you.

How is it they eventually came together?

It was in Sheng Siong, the most economical of local supermarkets, which had made them feel old—it'd been fourteen years, they were forty-one—and unglamourous. Arlene was out of her housing estate, ferrying her parents halfway across the island to a reputedly auspicious temple at their request. She'd left them to their own devices in the temple and had walked over to the supermarket in the neighbourhood centre for a bottle of mineral water. Her parents had not mentioned to her the two things they were praying for: the safe passage of an uncle who'd gone back to Xiamen to visit distant relatives, and that Arlene not be left on the shelf.

Nelly was in the condiments aisle, on her tippy toes, trying to get to a can of sardines.

Arlene saw her from the back, and though fourteen years had passed, she knew at once that it was Nelly. Her breath caught in her throat. Nelly had put on a little weight around the thighs and hips, and her hair had sparse greys in it. She was in sweat pants and a t-shirt.

Arlene walked right up behind Nelly as if in a dream, then reached over for the sardines.

Remember how we used to have this with bread in the middle of the night?

Nelly turned. Somehow, her face carried no surprise. She said: Arlene.

You wouldn't brush your teeth after, and your breath stank in the morning.

Arlene held up the can of sardines, and brought it down hard onto Nelly's right cheek, twice in quick succession. Nelly let out an involuntary cry as metal connected with bone. Shoppers stopped to stare, trolleys in tow. Arlene raised her hand again.

Arlene, Nelly said, her hand on her cheek, swelling a brilliant purple. Arlene, I left him.

Why had Nelly left her husband?

Arlene had never asked this of Nelly. Nelly thought this was grace on Arlene's part, but as time went by, she realised it was only because Arlene was hoping the reason was—her.

Nelly left her husband because he cheated on her, simple and banal. Nelly knew this reason would never be good enough for Arlene, and she feared the day Arlene would ask, but as it turned out, Arlene never did.

Did Arlene have any lovers in the (fourteen-year) interim?

No.

There were men who pursued Arlene for a time, but the consistency of her rejections would finally wear them down. Though plain, she was not unattractive, but she sought to downplay her looks.

She wore her hair in a dowdy crop that was neither feminine nor masculine, merely utilitarian. She steered clear of make-up, and stuck to a staple of neutral-coloured blouses and shirts tucked neatly into dark pants, paired with sensible shoes.

After just three years, the pursuits ceased altogether. As a teacher, it was easy to get stuck in the same routine, and the only new people she met were students.

She thought of getting a pet, but it was difficult for her to imagine forming attachments to a living thing. Finally, she taught herself to paint, from books. She was terrible in the beginning, but she kept at it, because she knew she needed something, any one thing, to hold on to, to invest in. After a year or two, she became fairly proficient with watercolours.

What did Arlene paint?

Arlene painted faceless women. That is, she painted women who were looking away from her, who had hair obscuring their face, who were reclined so far back their faces were never visible, whose profiles were in shadow, etc. There was always an excuse to call upon.

Outwardly, she told herself she did this because she couldn't paint faces to save her life—too much detail, she couldn't imagine rendering eyes, noses, lips. The lines of bodies soothed her. They weren't difficult to perfect, and it was faintly erotic to put finishing touches to breasts and thighs, observing the way light fell on the source paintings and sketches she used as references.

Inwardly, she knew that if she ever tried to paint a face, it would look like Nelly, and she could not afford to see Nelly ever again.

Did Arlene have sex in the interim?

No, but she subscribed to a virtual private network and

streamed ample amounts of independent Swedish porn.

Whenever she masturbated, she felt guilty. Not as a matter of prudence, but Arlene felt compelled to keep herself perfectly chaste. It wasn't that she thought Nelly would one day return to her. Arlene merely wanted to hold on to the certainty that she'd met the only person she wanted to emote to in this lifetime. That person had gone away, but Arlene thought that was a poor excuse to slip up in the emotional and physical sanctity of that certainty. She wouldn't even allow herself a cat. Arlene tended and guarded the altar of Nelly she had in her heart with care, in the manner of the most faithful, who have no prayers they want answered.

How long did it take Arlene's condition to deteriorate?

It took seven months before it became impossible to hide.

During these seven months, however, Arlene paid utmost attention to every last detail compounding Nelly. The spot of pigmentation at the tip of her left cheekbone that so bothered Nelly, but that was, really, barely more than a freckle. The differentials in the pitch of her sneeze, depending on whether it was her sinus or something more incidental.

Casually, she asked Nelly about *her* bucket list, which was conveniently short. Nelly was always a decisive woman. She laughed when Arlene came to her with the pencil and paper. She stroked the back of Arlene's neck: Are you afraid we're getting old? We're only fifty-two. I want to live till I'm a hundred and ten, with you. We've a whole life ahead of us.

They did what they could within those months—some were

simple enough: the tattoo of a crane, perpendicular to the base of Nelly's spine, a teenage whim that never materialised; a month's worth of a raw vegan diet, Nelly posing as Venus of Urbino on their living room floor, Arlene sketching her, trembling as she painted in the details of Nelly's face.

The trip to the Galápagos—two weeks, the longest they could reasonably afford during the June holidays—Nelly screaming in delight as a waved albatross nipped her ankle, running back to Arlene, having gone on ahead and sighted a bale of the famed giant tortoises. They could walk hand in hand as two women, fearless, in Ecuador. This was an unspoken part of the trip: to go somewhere far enough, that would be *safe* for them to be as they were. Here they pecked one another's cheeks on the cobblestone, on the coast, watched only by iguanas and mockingbirds. The days and nights seemed endless in the inn. They skipped the tour of Wolf Island on the last day to stay—quite alone—in the inn. As their fellow tourists pointed cameras at fur seals and vampire finches, Arlene and Nelly made covert love in the hot afternoon, buoyant in the deep-end of the kidney-shaped hotel pool, hands slipping under wet lycra.

Did Arlene get better?

Nelly rode in the ambulance with her, but when they got to the emergency room, the nurse asked if she was kin, and Nelly said slowly, No. *How are you related?* We're, we're friends. *I'm sorry ma'am, you'll have to wait outside then.* Nelly's fists were bunched up in the shape and size of her furious beating heart. She clenched and unclenched them, *lub dub lub dub*. The counter nurse was asking her to fill up a form with Arlene's particulars. She sat down on the blue plastic seats. The counter nurse was picking up the phone, calling immediate members of Arlene's family.

They'd spent so much of their life avoiding each other's family members, it was difficult being in the same room. It had never been conclusive, whether their Chinese-educated parents, both sets in their seventies by this point, understood the relations between Arlene and Nelly. Flatmates and childhood friends, they would say. Arlene's sister, seven years younger, duly married in her early twenties, had eased the pressure valve on Arlene when she delivered twin boys. The old woman's face was crumpled, the old man holding a trembling arm around her. No one spoke to Nelly. She excused herself to the bathroom, pulling down the lid of the WC and sitting there, wiping her eyes with toilet paper.

When she came back out, she saw the anguished huddle before the operating room, Arlene's mother clutching her husband for support. From afar, she saw the doctor shaking his head; Arlene's mother crumpling. Nelly's legs were giving way as she joined up, her movements mechanical. The doctor, in scrubs, was explaining the terminal condition and the complications in the surgery to Arlene's family.

I want to see her, Nelly said in a flat tone, splicing through Arlene's mother's sobs and the doctor's jargon. They turned to her in silent surprise. Arlene's sister was the first to regain her composure, snapping: How come you didn't know anything was wrong with her! You see her every day! The doctor was holding up his hands as if to say, I'm done here. He was untucking his shirt, gesturing to an attendant nurse to take over.

Was there a specific moment when, indeed, Nelly should have known that something was wrong?

Before they got into the kidney-shaped pool in the Galápagos, they were reclining in deck chairs, soaking up the Carribean sun. For once, Nelly wasn't obsessively reapplying sunblock to her pigmentation spot, or angling her visor to shield the most of her face. They were languid and laughing when Arlene said, *I could die happy here, right now.* Nelly looked over at Arlene and said: I wish we never had to leave.

What if we didn't?

You can't be serious.

Well, what if?

We'd need jobs.

We could teach English here. Or sell I Love Boobies *souvenir t-shirts on Avenue Charles Darwin.*

I'm sure the paperwork and permits are more complicated than that.

Yes, but I've never been happier.

Me too, Nelly said, and then she splashed some water onto Arlene with her foot. Arlene bent over and tickled Nelly till she couldn't breathe, they were both gasping with laughter, and then they went into the pool.

When Nelly thought back about it, she knew there was no point in blaming herself. These were things people said on holidays. What she did regret, though, was not asking Arlene what *her* bucket list was in turn, that evening at home on the couch.

The accompanying truth to this, though, was that, had she asked, Arlene would have told her that her—Nelly's—bucket list was, in fact, her—Arlene's—bucket list. That is to say, Arlene was happiest when she could service Nelly's wants. Arlene was happiest when Nelly was happy.

What happened after Arlene died?

It took half a year.

For?

For Nelly to reconnect with her ex-husband. It started non-descript and easy, the ataraxia of email, progressing on to the natural gratification of catching up over coffee, once they'd both ascertained that the other was no longer with the alleged previous lover, for whatever reasons, a point of conversation they fudged copiously, complicit. It'd been seven and a half years; it was easy to let things slide, to find graceless yet intransigent comfort in that old, disenchanting familiarity. Nelly was fifty-three and her husband was fifty-five, neither held the illusion that they had better long-term options. Neither spoke about the gulf of the seven and a half years—Nelly kept mum about Arlene, and her ex-husband never once-mentioned the ex-mistress's name. They regarded each other, from separate far ends of the impassable gulf, comfortably. They re-married in a quiet civil ceremony and remained childlessly, placidly together till the end of their days.

Why would anyone title this The Ballad of Arlene & Nelly?
They would do so for Arlene.

For Arlene?
The deaths—tiny ones, false ones, real ones—we undertake in the name of love are the closest that we ever come to greatness.